Age
of
Consent

Age of Consent

MARK THOMPSON

Heliotrope Books

New York

978-1-956474-79-4
978-1-956474-78-7– eBook

Heliotrope Books LLC
heliotropebooks@gmail.com

Cover Photo courtesy of Mark Thompson

Designed and typeset by Heliotrope Books

For Cathy, again

Also by Mark Thompson:

What Makes a Man Run

"My bounty is as boundless as the sea,
My love as deep. The more I give to thee,
The more I have, for both are infinite."

—*Shakespeare,* **Romeo and Juliet**

1978

SEPTEMBER 1978

On the first day of school, Rusty learns about the new English teacher. At his locker, he overhears a senior who's on the football team say, "I've got this new teacher for English, and man, she's fucking hot!" Rusty listens for more about this but hears nothing. He moves away from his locker and looks up and down the hallway over the throngs of students heading to their next classes, but the senior and whoever he was talking to have gone.

In the cafeteria during lunch, his best friend, Larry, says, "Hey, I heard there's some foxy new English teacher here."

Rusty looks up from his turkey sandwich. "Yeah, I heard something about that. You've seen her?"

"Nah."

On his way to his next class, he hears another upperclassman ask, "Hey, did you check out the new teacher?"

It's a small school, but for the rest of the day, Rusty doesn't see anyone who might be her. Rusty only knows that his own English teacher, Mr. Consalvo, a slight bearded wisp of a man, does not fit the description. By the time the final bell rings at two o'clock, Rusty has forgotten about it.

Today is also the first day of practice for the Northfield High School cross-country team. Rusty Rasmussen, or "Raz," as he's sometimes called, is sitting on the grass next to the track, doing stretches. Shaggy-haired and shirtless, like many of his fellow teammates, he's already dripping with sweat after the mile warmup that the team captain Michael Wiseman has just demanded of them. It's a hot and humid late-summer midafternoon. Across the track from where they sit is the football field, where players are being hectored by their coaches as they run plays or slam into tackling dummies. Down at the other end of the track, pretty girls in shorts and tee shirts carry pompoms and practice cheerleading routines.

Wiseman is now having the team do the "butterfly stretch," in which the runner sits knees out, with the feet are joined together. Rusty pushes down on his thighs to stretch his groin muscles when he sees Coach Kirschner approach on his left with a young woman in tow.

At the sight of her, an erotic jolt courses through his body. She's of medium height with wavy brown shoulder-length hair and tan skin. She wears blue running shorts with white trim and a red T-shirt that reveals an ample chest. Rusty turns to Larry and asks, "Hey, Larry, does the coach have a girlfriend?"

Larry snorts. "Are you kidding me? Who would fuck him?"

"Well, who's that over there with him?"

"Whoa!"

As she approaches, she reminds Rusty of the actress Susan Sarandon in the Louis Malle film *Pretty Baby*, a movie Rusty was unable to see due to his parents' prohibition against him seeing movies with strong sexual content. However, he's seen pictures of Sarandon in *Variety* and is impressed by her beauty. But as the woman draws near, Rusty can see that her features are different from Sarandon's. She has wide turquoise eyes, a large nose, high cheekbones, and an olive complexion. She's not the typical WASP predominant here in Northfield. Where on earth did she come from?

The two finally reach the team and patiently wait as they finish stretching. Kirschner is a man of medium height with short curly red hair, which has earned him the nickname "Eraser Head." Larry has told Rusty that Kirschner is a whack job, but Rusty doesn't see that. A bit high-strung maybe, but not nutso.

When they finish stretching, Kirschner says, "Okay guys, I hope you all had a good summer and got in some good training. I've got someone to introduce here. This is Ms. Levy, she's a new English teacher, and she'll be assisting me with the girls."

So that was her!

Larry leans over to Rusty, "You have her for English?"

"No, do you?"

"No."

Rusty turns to look at Ms. Levy. "Too bad," he says.

"Today, we're going to do an eight-mile run" Rusty hears some quiet groans from some of his teammates, including Larry. Eight miles is a bit of a stretch for Rusty, but he's too distracted to care.

* * * * *

An hour later, Rusty and his new teammates are out for their first team run through the streets of Northfield, a small well-to-do community in south-central Fairfield County, Connecticut. It's a picturesque town of stone walls, barns converted to some other purpose, and old colonial-era houses. Undeveloped areas are mostly woodland that will soon become spectacular with the upcoming fall foliage. The beauty of the place tends to be lost on teenagers like Rusty, who view smaller towns like Northfield as being "hick towns," though there is actually no one living here who could be described as a "hick." These are towns that offer teens nothing much to do.

Rusty is fifteen years old and a sophomore. At six feet three inches, he's tall, with a thatch of red hair. His first name is Peter, but he gave himself the nickname "Rusty," naming himself after his favorite baseball player, a similarly red-haired third baseman named Rusty Staub of the New York Mets. Only his mother continues to call him "Peter."

This is his first year as a cross-country runner. He's joined the team at the urging of his track coach, Anthony Scarpella, who argued forcefully and persuasively that running cross-country would get him in good shape for the winter indoor and spring outdoor track seasons.

Rusty's by himself, trailing the lead pack of runners, his friend Larry among them. Larry's also a sophomore, though he is a year older than Rusty, having been held back a year in middle school. He alone of Rusty's teammates is built like a football player, yet he's managed to run a sub five-minute mile with minimal training and much alcohol abuse. Rusty wonders how that can be possible. It's unfair!

Whenever Rusty runs, or in another situation when his mind is free to wander, some song usually plays in his head, and today's song is "Boogie, Oogie, Oogie," by A Taste of Honey, a tune that's been getting constant airplay, particularly on AM radio. It doesn't matter that Rusty is no fan of disco ("Disco sucks!" is the common refrain in these parts); if he's heard the song recently on the radio, it sticks to his head like flypaper.

Rusty decides to distract himself and get rid of the song, so he surges toward the group. They are now on Northfield Road, on a seemingly endless uphill section of the run. He wonders what his pace is: five, six, seven minutes a mile, he has no clue. He has no stopwatch, just a Timex wristwatch, and there are no mile markers. You're either jogging or running hard, or in this case running hard or running fucking hard. With difficulty, he manages to catch up to the rest of the group, who are mainly upperclassmen. They're talking about Ms. Levy.

"Think she's married?" asks a senior named Curt.

"What does it matter? She ain't banging you!" retorts Larry, causing laughter from the group.

"Why don't women teachers sleep with us? Guy teachers do it all the time," says John, a fellow sophomore.

"No, only Mr. Goodbar does that," says Wayne, a junior, referring to Mr. Johnston, a math teacher who happens to be the boys' varsity basketball coach. He's a notorious rake who dresses like an actor auditioning for *Saturday Night Fever* with his bell-bottomed trousers, shirts unbuttoned at the top revealing ample amounts of chest hair and gold chains, and a handlebar mustache. Rusty can easily imagine him cruising the singles bars at night after pursuing teenage girls in the daytime. "Anyway," continues Wayne, "girls like her don't stay single for very long. If she ain't married, she most likely has a boyfriend her age or older."

"I wouldn't let that stop me," John replies.

"You're not ready for primetime," says Michael Wiseman. "Sixteen is the age of consent here in Connecticut."

"You know this from personal experience?" asks Larry, eliciting laughter from Rusty and the rest of the group.

"My dad is a lawyer. He defended a teacher like Mr. Goodbar. He got off, so to speak."

General hilarity follows. Then Michael says, "Anyway, I don't know what you guys see in this Ms. Levy. She's got these big froggy eyes, and her nose is too big."

"Yeah, but Raz is in love with her," says Larry.

Wiseman turns to Rusty with a grin. "That true, Raz?"

"Yeah, I think she's hot. What about it?"

The conversation drifts on to other topics as they turn onto the predictably named School Road for the final half mile to the high school. They run up to a side door in the high school building that leads to the locker rooms. Ms. Levy is there, holding court with a group of girl runners. She seems to be hitting it off with them. Rusty and his teammates are silent as they file past her and enter the building. She'll definitely be in his thoughts tonight when he pleasures himself before sleep.

* * * * *

Rusty sits in the passenger side of Larry's Chevy Blazer, gripping hard against the side panels of the door, wondering if he's going to survive his ride home. He's glad for the ride. He usually misses the late bus after workouts, and Larry's car beats waiting for his mom to get out of work at five or walking two miles home after a workout. A ride means he'll be home for an extra hour to do homework and to feed and walk his dog, a border collie named Duffy. However, as Larry rounds a sharp curve at 50 m.p.h. (the posted speed limit is 25), Rusty begins to wonder it's worth risking death at age fifteen, and worse yet, dying a virgin.

Larry's father, a vice president of sales for IBM, bought the vehicle for him when he got his driver's license. Rusty wonders if his father knew how Larry drove if he'd take away his car. At least this car has FM radio. Rusty's dad, frugal to the extreme, has always felt AM/FM car radios are an unnecessary extravagance, so Rusty's had to settle for the pop music offered by AM music stations. Now at least, he's being treated to "Hot Blooded" by Foreigner, a song that makes him think of Ms. Levy.

Larry makes a sharp right turn on a steep downhill onto Rusty's street. He guns the engine, and it takes seconds for them to cover the quarter mile to a driveway that several homes share. A left turn on that, and Larry floors it one last time on the downhill driveway. Rusty's house is the last one on the right, and it has a sharp downhill slope. Rusty closes his eyes, bracing for impact, perhaps against the metal pole that holds the basketball net. But somehow, Larry manages to bring the car to a stop at the end of the driveway.

"Enjoy your ride?" asks Larry, laughing.

Rusty takes a breath. "It's good to be alive."

"So, what are you up to?"

"Gotta walk the dog, then homework. Back to the fucking grind. You?"

"Probably get a fifth of Southern Comfort and get fucked up."

Rusty regards him for a moment. He's long suspected that Larry might have a problem with booze, and possibly drugs as well. His family life seems a bit dicey, with divorced parents and a much younger sister with her own issues. Larry's never asked Rusty to accompany him on his misadventures, which is probably a good thing, but also puzzling as well. He wants to say something to Larry, that he is concerned about him, but he doesn't want to be preachy. Finally, in a jokey manner, Rusty says, "You should lay off that shit. You'd probably kick my ass running if you stopped."

"I kick your ass running anyway."

It was true. "Yeah, later dude." Rusty slams the car door shut and fishes out his garage door key as Larry wheels his car around and speeds back up the driveway. Fucking guy is a danger on the road.

Rusty enters his house, a green two-story colonial, via the basement, and there is his dog, Duffy, coming at him full sprint. Rusty kneels down and embraces his dog, feeling his hot breath and wet tongue lap against his face. He imagines what it would be like to have Ms. Levy, or better yet, Mrs. Rasmussen, his lawfully wedded wife, greet him at the door after a hard day's work.

* * * * *

Rusty is the youngest of two children. His sister, Patti, eleven years his senior, lives in Manhattan, pursuing an acting career. He was born just outside Chicago and lived there with his family until his father, a commercial architect, accepted a position in New York City when Rusty was six. They have lived in Northfield ever since.

Rusty sits in his bedroom, playing his guitar, his way of unwinding after doing homework. His repertoire is a mix of songs from the sixties from bands like The Beatles and The Rolling Stones, plus more recent material from acts like Lynyrd Skynyrd and The Eagles. Though he takes guitar lessons and is diligent in practicing, it's not a serious passion for Rusty. He has no ambitions to be in a band or a solo performer. It's just a way of relaxing and passing the time.

"Peter! Time for dinner," his mother shouts from downstairs. Rusty scampers down the stairs to the kitchen where he greets his father, Jim, who has just finished his daily commute to and from Manhattan. He, like Rusty, is tall, with thick blond hair and clear blue eyes. He's of Nordic descent. Rusty's mother, Dolores, is a woman of medium height and build with brown hair and a slightly darker complexion than his father's. She's of Polish descent. They met when they were college students at the University of Illinois.

Dinner follows the usual script. After the food has been served, in this case a sumptuous dish of spaghetti and meat balls, a one-way conversation occurs, with Dolores chatting away about events at work. She's a legal secretary, working for a local lawyer who specializes in real estate and divorce cases. Dolores is fairly new at this work. She has recently finished secretarial school and has taken this job to pay for Rusty's college education. She clearly is fascinated by her new job, and Jim, a taciturn man to begin with, is unable to utter a single syllable—or maybe he's happy not to. Rusty doesn't even have to excuse himself as he heads to the kitchen to serve himself seconds. For Rusty, between his teenage metabolism and his cross-country workouts, food is fuel, something to be consumed as soon and as often as possible, without any distractions.

Rusty's about to finish his second helping when his father turns to him and asks, "How was your day today?"

Time to engage in conversation. "Well, we had our first day of cross-country practice."

"How did that go?"

"It was hard. Not easy to keep up with Larry and the rest of the guys on the team."

"Well, you've never run long distances until recently," his mom points out.

"That's true. Anyway, the other interesting thing was that Coach Kirschner has an assistant coach now. Some beautiful new English teacher named Ms. Levy."

"Why does he need an assistant coach?" his father asks.

"To help out on the girls' end," replies Rusty, getting up to help himself to thirds.

"You say she's an English teacher?"

"Yep. Very young, and pretty."

"Is she one of your teachers?"

My, my, thinks Rusty: he's suddenly inquisitive for a quiet guy. That's the funny thing about him. When the conversation involves women or girls, Dad becomes a different man.

"No, I don't have her."

"That's too bad."

"Jim!" says his mom, in an admonishing tone.

His dad looks down at his dinner, stifling a laugh.

* * * * *

Travis Wilson, Rusty's guitar teacher, is the sort of guy who could be the subject of a country song. A large, bearded, barrel-chested man in his mid-thirties, he's a veteran of several rock and country bands of varying levels of success. Married and divorced, with two kids to help support, he's been taking on students to supplement his income at a nearby wire factory. Travis teaches from his home in Georgetown, a community only ten minutes away, so it's not too inconvenient for his mom to take him there.

Rusty enjoys his lessons with Travis. Travis regales him with stories of life on the road, including scenes of drug and alcohol abuse, sex with groupies and other tales of debauchery that would scandalize Rusty's socially conservative parents, particularly since they're paying for his lessons. Still, his parents get their money's worth for two reasons. One, Travis is a knowledgeable teacher, and two, Rusty is conscientious about practicing.

They're working on a rock song by Bad Company called "Feel Like Making Love." Rusty finds it to be a tricky tune, since it transitions from a country ballad to a real rock interlude during the chorus with that big power chord which is the centerpiece of the song, and power chords are not his strong point on guitar.

"Man, you're putting some effort into that," marvels Travis. "Is there some girl you have in mind when you try to play it?"

Rusty laughs. "Yeah. Not a girl though. A woman."

"Oh! Some TV actress?"

"No, this new teacher at my school."

"You've got a hot teacher now?" Travis is very interested.

"She's not my teacher. I don't have her. She's an English teacher who's the girls' cross-country coach, which is kinda odd, since she doesn't have a distance runner's body, really."

"Describe her to me," says Travis.

"Hmm...okay. Medium height, brown hair, shoulder length, kinda frizzy. She has a killer body."

"Yeah?" Replies Travis, his eyebrows elevating.

"Yeah, um...very curvaceous," Rusty replies with a grin. "Olive complexion, interesting face. She's got these huge eyes."

"Is she married?"

"I don't think so. We call her Ms. Levy, not Mrs. Levy."

"Ah, so she's Jewish," observes Travis.

"Yeah, I guess so," Rusty replies. "We have some Jewish kids, teachers too. None of them look anything like her."

"Well, let's get back to work on those power chords," says Travis. "The way to a woman's heart is to play her some music."

* * * * *

Rusty stands at the end of his driveway on a warm Friday evening, waiting for Larry to pick him up. His mind wanders randomly among various subjects: his schoolwork, cross-country training, and Ms. Levy. He thinks about approaching her sometime, maybe striking up a conversation. What would they talk about? Maybe running. She's an English teacher, so maybe they can talk about books?

Just then, Rusty sees headlights of a vehicle speeding up the road. Has to be Larry, no one else drives like that. The Chevy Blazer skids to a stop, and Rusty pauses for a moment to make sure the car is not going anywhere before approaching it. "Hey," says Larry as Rusty hops in.

"What's up?"

"We're gonna do something different tonight," says Larry as he puts the vehicle in gear.

"What's that?" Rusty asks with trepidation.

"We're gonna play floor hockey," says Larry as he presses down hard on the accelerator, causing the tires to squeal and the car to take off like a fighter jet from an aircraft carrier.

"We're going to do what?"

"Floor hockey. I went to the elementary school gym this afternoon, and I propped a window open. I think I can get my body through it, so I can let everyone in the building.

"You *think* you can get your body through?" asks Rusty, appalled. "That's the most fucked up idea you've come up with."

Larry drives his Chevy Blazer to the high school parking lot. A couple of cars are parked there with several kids hanging out, a typical scene on an eventless weekend evening.

Rusty gets out of the car and notices a pungent odor that's foreign to him. "What's that smell?" he asks.

Larry laughs. "That's weed, you fucking idiot."

They approach the kids, who number about a half dozen. One of them, a stoner named Rob Desmond asks, "We still on for floor hockey?"

"Yeah, let's go. I can get you guys inside."

"Well, all fucking right then!" The kids pile into their respective vehicles and tear down School Road to the elementary school. Rusty still thinks that this is a stupid idea, but in a town with not much to do, you have to invent your own fun.

The small caravan arrives at the elementary school parking lot. The kids pile out and Larry leads everyone to the window, which is still propped open. Rob asks, "You think you can get through that?"

"Yeah, no problem," he replies, though his tone betrays an uncertainty. The bottom of the window is six feet up, and there's not much space to crawl through. When Larry tries to hoist himself up, he can't get through. Rusty has an idea.

"Larry, try it this way." Rusty has his hands together, palms up, fingers interlocked. Larry steps on the offered hands and this time is able to have enough leverage to work his way through. It's still difficult. Rusty belatedly realizes that a thinner kid like himself would have had an easier time of it, but Larry is eventually able to squeeze his frame through the open window and plop down on the other side. Rusty and the others run to the front entrance.

Larry opens the door, and everyone runs inside. It's strange being inside these hallways, familiar from his childhood, now dark and empty. They enter the gym, and Larry turns on the lights. The space hasn't changed a bit.

They rush to a supply closet and raid the treasure trove of plastic hockey sticks, nets and a puck. The boys place the nets on opposite sides of the gym and then choose sides. Larry places the puck square in the middle, and then play begins.

Throughout his youth, Rusty hated floor hockey. He was never very good at it, and he frequently got hurt, mostly the result of his exposed shins being struck by the stick blades. But that was in gym class. The blue jeans he's now wearing give him some protection, and this allows him to be less tentative and more aggressive while playing. He doesn't mind getting body checked, and he in turn dishes out some good hits of his own. At one point, he gets the puck, and after weaving around a couple of players like Bobby Orr, he shoots and scores a goal.

Right after that, a male voice booms out, "Well, well, well...what do we have here?"

Rusty and his fellow players turn and see six members of the Northfield Police Department standing at the gym's entrance.

Well, duh, Rusty thinks. Of course, we'd get busted. The police station is across the athletic fields from the school building. They could see that the gym lights were on and decided to come over and check things out.

"How did you guys get in here?" one of the cops asks.

Rusty points at the open window. "One of us crawled through that."

"So, you guys didn't break in. Okay, then. We won't arrest you, but we're taking you kids home."

"But we have cars, we can drive home!" Larry protests.

"Oh, no, we insist. You're coming with us. First, you'll put back the hockey equipment."

Dejected though relieved that they're not in bigger trouble (the police apparently are not searching anyone's vehicle), Rusty and his fellow players do as they are told before they are each assigned a cop who will take them home. Rusty is assigned to Treadwell, a tall and beefy specimen with a brush mustache, who leads him to his squad car. When Rusty enters, he marvels at vehicle's interior, especially the two-way radio.

"Where to, kid?" the cop asks.

Rusty gives him his address. Geez, the cops here don't have much to do either if they're able to act as a taxi service. Rusty directs the cop to his house. When they arrive, Rusty says, "Thanks officer. Have a good night."

"Just a minute, I have to go with you. I have to talk to your folks."

"Oh." Now this is going to be awkward and embarrassing. He and the cop exit the car and walk together to the front door. Rusty pushes the doorbell, and within a minute, Rusty's parents appear, both with alarmed expressions. They were not expecting any visitors at 10 pm, let alone a police officer with their son in his custody.

"Mr. and Mrs. Rasmussen?"

"Yes," replies his mom.

"I'm just bringing your son home. We found him and some other kids playing floor hockey in the elementary school gym, which is closed and off limits."

The facial expressions of his parents could not be more different. His mom looks appalled, his dad is visibly stifling a laugh.

"Oh, honestly, how could you? Why were you in there in the first place?"

Rusty shrugs. "I don't know, guess we were bored."

"Go upstairs, Peter. I'll talk to you later."

As Rusty enters the house, his father grins and winks at him. He goes upstairs and hears his mom apologize to the cop. He enters his room and shuts the door, awaiting a scolding that never comes.

Guess dad must have talked to her.

OCTOBER 1978

On a cool and crisp October morning, Coach Kirschner has the runners out at 8:00 am on a Saturday, on the Northfield High School track. This workout promises to be especially hellish, an interval workout of eight 880-yard runs. That's four miles of hard running. The workout is bad enough, but to schedule this workout at 8 am seems especially heinous.

Rusty looks around and doesn't see Larry. He probably decided to sleep this one out. Most of Rusty's teammates look pretty bleary-eyed, the one exception being the team captain, Michael Wiseman, who appears ready to crush this workout. Must be nice to be a morning person.

Through the haze of his fatigue, Rusty can make out snippets of conversation, mainly about how the New York Yankees are doing. They have been a frequent topic of conversation, particularly since their shortstop Bucky Dent hit a three-run homer in the special American League East tiebreaker game against the Boston Red Sox. The conversations are of limited interest to Rusty since he's a Mets fan.

"Okay, guys," Coach Kirschner begins in his whiny voice. "We're going to jog a few laps to warm up before we begin the workout. Let's get this started so we can get this over with." Rusty and his teammates shuffle over to the track and begin to jog. Off to the side of the track is Ms. Levy, dressed in her form-fitting blue and white Adidas sweatpants and jacket. Rusty feels a nudge to his left.

"Hey Raz, your girlfriend is here," says Michael Wiseman, grinning.

"God, if only that were true."

Wiseman gives him a good-natured shove but says nothing further. Rusty has sensed a decency in Michael, who wouldn't rag on him for admitting his feelings for a teacher. Michael's response has confirmed Rusty's intuition. It also helps that Larry isn't around to overhear this brief conversation.

After jogging a listless mile on the track and the mandatory stretching and calisthenics, the runners shuffle zombielike to the starting line. *How the fuck am I going to run eight hard half-milers?* "You've never done this workout before, have you?" says Michael Wiseman to Rusty.

"No, nothing like this."

"I'd go easy at first. You don't want to get fried after your first couple of repeats. Don't worry about how fast you're going or what everyone else is doing. If you feel strong when you run the last one, then you can gun it. Not until then."

"Oh, okay. Thanks."

Kirshner has the boys line up in front. The girls behind will be starting thirty seconds later, Ms. Levy will be timing them. Rusty finds it difficult to take his eyes off her, even at the onset of a tough workout.

"Okay guys, everyone up on the starting line. Ready, set, go!"

Rusty watches Wiseman and the faster runners on the team surge ahead as he settles into what feels like a manageable pace. I just want to survive this fucking workout, he reminds himself. As he nears the completion of each lap, he notices Ms. Levy either glancing at him, or even staring at him. The surge of excitement is enough to cause Rusty to momentarily forget his fatigue, even though he's becoming more out of breath with each repeat. He's running his intervals in the mid 2:30's, a far cry from his personal best of 2:08, but even a novice like Rusty knows you can't compare an all-out race time with an interval workout.

Finally, they come to the eighth and final interval. Rusty feels strong enough for a more aggressive effort. Once Kirschner sends them off, Rusty runs the first lap fast enough to keep Wiseman within striking distance—about ten yards ahead. Rusty completes the first lap, and he hears the Coach cry out "1:17, 1:18." Rusty mounts a sprint, gradually gaining on Wiseman. By the time they reach the far turn, Rusty is right behind him. He stays behind Wiseman until they come to the final straightaway before mounting his surge. Wiseman stays even with Rusty until the final ten yards, when Rusty finds another gear and surges ahead. When Rusty crosses the line, he hears Kirschner yell out "2:29!"

Rusty bends down, his hands on his knees as he gasps for breath. He hears Ms. Levy say, "Good job, Rusty!" Rusty turns to her and smiles. He feels a nudge on his right. He turns and sees Wiseman flashing a smile.

* * * * *

The school bell rings for the final time of the day. Rusty leaves his U.S. history class, makes his way through the gaggle of students, and heads to his locker. He dials the combination, opens his locker, throws his notebook and textbook inside, and slams it shut. Next, he begins his stroll to the boys' gym locker room, passing groups of kids gossiping, couples openly making out, kids hurrying to buses waiting out front, and others like Rusty, on their way to after-school activities.

As he nears the gym locker room, Rusty notices a group of larger boys in a semicircle. They wear the blue and gold varsity jackets that are ubiquitous among the athletically inclined juniors and seniors. In about a year, Rusty will get one of these jackets.

There's something menacing about this gathering. They have cornered a kid named Daniel Krakowski, a short, pudgy, sloppily-dressed boy with severe acne and a quiet demeanor. Throughout his time here, Rusty has heard other students describe Daniel as ugly, an idiot, and a loser. Daniel is a junior, and Rusty has never met him. Nor has he ever had a class with him.

But Rusty tenses up as he watches the upperclassmen on the football team hurl insults, and occasionally shove Daniel, and it all becomes too much for him to bear. It reminds Rusty of a painful past that is not too distant. But what can he do? He's not a good fighter. There are at least a half dozen of them, and Rusty couldn't even beat the weakest of them individually. Confronting them isn't an option, but he just can't let this go on, even though the idea of intervening terrifies him. But then an idea comes to him.

He walks over to Daniel, as if he's a good buddy of his. Daniel is cowering, his back against a wall. Forcing a smile, Rusty yells "Danny, how's it going? I need to talk to you about something…" Rusty feels a hard shove coming from his left, and he nearly loses his balance.

"We're talking to him, asshole," growls one of the football players. Shocked and suddenly scared, Rusty throws his hands up to convey a "Hey, what the fuck?" kind of gesture.

"Hey, whatcha doing there?" It is a loud, sharp female voice, delivered in a pronounced New York accent, with the authority that can only come from a teacher. Everyone involved is startled. Rusty turns to look. It's Ms. Levy.

She strides over to the football players like a cop confronting a gang of hoodlums. Gone is the sweet assistant to Coach Kirschner. In her place is someone Rusty had no idea existed. "Hey tough guys, we gotta problem here? You want me to send you to the principal's office?" The contempt in her voice is palpable.

"Uh, no," responds one of the offending jocks, his eyes wide open.

"Then move!" They quickly disperse. Ms. Levy walks over to Daniel. "Are you okay?" she asks, her tone much quieter. He silently nods his head and looks downward. Rusty turns and resumes his journey to the locker room. "Hey Rusty, wait up!" Ms Levy calls out, trotting toward him. "Are you all right?"

"Yeah, sure."

"You know that kid?"

"Well, no actually, not really."

Ms. Levy's large turquoise eyes somehow manage to widen further. "You stood up for a guy you don't even know?"

Rusty feels embarrassed somehow. "Well, yeah, I guess."

"That's really wonderful, I'm proud of you!"

Rusty can feel himself blushing. "Well, you were pretty good yourself just now," he replies, trying to deflect the attention.

"Hey, I'm Brooklyn born and bred, baby!" she says smiling. "My first teaching gig was in the South Bronx. These guys here are creampuffs!" She playfully punches Rusty in the arm. "I'll see you at practice."

He has never felt so revved up before a workout.

* * * * *

Rusty and his teammates are on a school bus that takes them to an "away meet" in Newtown, a community in the northern part of the county. He's keyed up for this race, far more so than for any previous competition, for the start and finish will take place in Bruce Jenner Stadium, a facility named after the Olympic decathlon champion who had attended Newtown High. Jenner is Rusty's athletic hero. He was a pimply faced thirteen-year-old boy in braces when he saw Jenner run, jump and throw his way to the Olympic gold medal, and he was awestruck. To Rusty, Jenner was, and is, the epitome of masculinity. It wasn't enough to be like Bruce Jenner, Rusty wanted to *be* Bruce Jenner. Rusty was struck by his mane of chestnut brown hair, his angelic face, and his muscular body that wanted to explode from his blood red USA singlet and his tight-fitting blue and white Adidas shorts. I bet I could get any girl I wanted if

I looked like him, Rusty reasoned. He immediately became interested in track and field.

The following spring, after being cut from the middle school basketball team tryouts that winter, Rusty went out for track. In his first meet, a dual meet with another middle school, Rusty won the 880-yard run and the high jump and took second in the long jump. At last, he'd found something he was kind of good at! It was a happy ending to what was an otherwise miserable middle school experience.

Alas, Rusty will eventually discover that he doesn't have a decathlete's body. He lacks the upper body strength to be a good thrower and the gymnastic ability necessary to be a successful pole vaulter. He does have enough spring in his legs to be a decent at the high jump and the long jump. But he really shows potential as a runner. Rusty lacks the explosive speed to be a sprinter like Houston McTear, currently the fastest man on the planet. But he can run well over longer distances, as he happily discovered. With a little bit of training, Rusty found that he could tolerate the two minutes or so of shortness of breath that is part and parcel of running a half mile, and he could beat most kids his age while doing so. After an unhappy season as a bench warmer on the boy's freshman soccer team, Rusty committed himself entirely to cross-country and track. He feels it's a good fit for a physically active kid who sucks at team sports.

The bus driver puts the radio on, and above the voices of Larry and his other teammates, Rusty can hear the song "Kiss You All Over" by Exile. The song is the subject of much adolescent snickering, which Rusty has joined from time to time to be one of the boys. But when he hears the song, either on the radio or in his head, he imagines himself making love to the actress Cheryl Ladd, a star on the TV show *Charlie's Angels*, or Valerie Bertinelli from *One Day at a Time*. Lately, Ms. Levy has been part of his fantasy mix.

Over the past few weeks, he has noticed her in the hallways in between classes, in addition to cross-country practice and meets, and occasionally they acknowledge each other in passing. He's heard that she's an engaging teacher, has rather tough standards, but is fair. She's certainly very popular with the students, particularly the boys. Hordes of jock upperclassmen follow her like a school of sharks, trying to flirt with her. She seems to enjoy the attention, but she doesn't seem particularly drawn to them. The kids she does seem drawn to, oddly enough, are the stoners, girls as well as boys, particularly those who are academically or artistically inclined.

Rusty's also noticed that she's made a friend on the faculty, Mrs. Kingsley, a fetching young blond who's a gym teacher and the girl's volleyball coach. Rusty has long observed that the more glamorous girls in his school tend to hang out with each other. You never see a good-looking girl pal up with an ugly one. This appears to be true in the adult world as well.

As the bus rumbles along, Rusty cranes his head to get a look at Ms. Levy. There she is, a few rows up, talking with Mr. Kirschner, who sits to her left, presumably talking strategy. On the radio, he hears Exile's lead singer implore his lover to show him everything she does and that no one does it quite like her.

The bus suddenly turns left, and there they are at the parking lot of Newtown High School. Rusty has an involuntary erection, but since he's wearing loose fitting sweatpants over his running shorts, he's not concerned. The bus comes to a stop, its door swings open, and everyone piles out. A couple of Newtown runners greet them. They are the captains of the boys' and girls' teams, and they're here to give the visiting team a tour of the course. Greetings are exchanged between the coaches and the captains of both teams. Rusty notices the boys' captain is agog at the sight of Ms. Levy.

The team follows the Newtown captains as they walk across the parking lot. Within a minute they are at the place Rusty has been dreaming about, Bruce Jenner Stadium.

"You fucking call this a stadium? You can't be serious," says Larry incredulously.

Rusty can't help but snigger. It's a typical high school athletic complex, a football field with a scoreboard at one end, surrounded by a cinder track, the same as Northfield. It has more bleachers than Northfield, a lot more, in fact. But it hardly passes for a stadium. Nonetheless, a sign above the scoreboard proudly proclaims this spot as "Bruce Jenner Stadium."

So this is where he started on his journey to become the world's greatest athlete! Rusty feels newly energized, despite his somewhat disappointing surroundings.

Now the Newtown captains take the Northfield runners on a tour of the course. This seems to Rusty a useless exercise. There's no way he can remember the route, with all its twists, turns and detours. He wonders how a far superior runner from a visiting team would fare. He or she would either need a photographic memory or would have to run with the lead runner for the host team—and then sprint ahead when the finish line was in sight.

After the tour is over, Rusty and his teammates jog a couple of laps in the stadium. He imagines himself as Jenner, leading his teammates on a warm-up run, before crushing his competition in all the events he competes in, and taking Ms. Levy into his arms. Once the jogging is done, the captains lead the runners in stretching exercises. First the hamstrings, then the "Hurdler's Stretch" for the quads, the groin stretches, and so on.

Finally, it's time for the runners to report to the starting line. Rusty feels strong and confident that he will run well. That crazy Saturday morning 8 x 880-yard workout that Kirschner had everyone do seems to have worked wonders for him. Maybe I should do that more often, Rusty thinks. Approaching the line, he sees the Newtown runners are already there, and runners from both teams jog in place, jump up and down, and even do wind sprints. The autumn air is crisp and cold, an ideal afternoon for a cross-country race.

A middle-aged man, who Rusty remembers is the opposing team's coach, is serving as the starter. He gathers all the runners together, telling them "Okay people, just one command. I'll say 'Runners ready,' then the gun."

The runners line up on a line drawn on the dirt track. "RUNNERS READY?" A starter's pistol goes off.

Rusty starts off slowly, letting the faster runners pass, including his friend Larry. He follows the leaders as they exit the stadium on an uphill path, and into a parking lot. Then they enter an athletic field, with Newtown football players practicing. They stop their scrimmaging to glower at them, but they say nothing. That's an improvement from the players from Central Catholic, who openly taunted them, challenging the Northfield runners to fight them. What dicks!

Rusty follows a Newtown runner into a forested area. Now they are running on a trail. It has some steep ups and downs, but it doesn't seem to affect Rusty at all. He feels strong, his legs responding well to the sudden challenges of the course, and he feels no fatigue or shortness of breath.

He gains on the Newtown runner. Rusty is reluctant to pass him, because he's been using him as a guide. Farther ahead, he sees Larry. He could pass this guy and follow Larry, but that seems to Rusty a dicey proposition, since *Larry* might end up losing his way. But then on a straightaway, Rusty can make out another Newtown runner ahead of Larry. All right then!

Rusty surges ahead of the Newtown runner, and now he has his sights on his friend. The trail makes a sharp right-hand turn, and Rusty guesses that they are at the halfway point. Larry is about twenty yards ahead. He looks strong, but Rusty gains on him, slowly, gradually, but getting closer nonetheless.

The trail ends, now they're back on the fields, passing a girls' field hockey practice. No glares or taunts from them. Next, they're back in the parking lot, and there up ahead is Bruce Jenner Stadium. He's only five yards behind Larry.

Rusty follows Larry down a path to the track inside the "stadium." He thinks of his hero, BRUCE! He knows they run only half a lap before they reach the finish. Time to gun it. Rusty picks up the pace, his lungs desperately trying to bring in air. He draws even with Larry, who glances at him, his face cast in a shocked expression. He tries to stay with Rusty, but Rusty surges ahead, and Larry gives up. Rusty rounds the final turn and sprints to the finish. He hears Ms. Levy yell, "C'mon Rusty, go for it!" Yes! He crosses the line and doubles over, hands on his knees, panting furiously.

He finds out that he finished in 5th place overall and was the 3rd Northfield runner to cross the line.

* * * *

They are on the bus ride home, the sky rapidly becoming darker. Rusty feels elated over his stellar race. Larry has taken it well, though he has taken some ribbing from some of the other teammates. Rusty sits behind Coach Kirschner. He seems to be having some discussion with the upperclassmen, particularly with Michael Wiseman, the team captain who is likely to be the class valedictorian and is aspiring to get into Harvard. The talk doesn't appear to involve running. As he leans forward to eavesdrop, Rusty learns it's about the end of the Second World War, specifically about whether it was necessary to drop the atomic bomb on Japan. Kirschner is clearly against it.

"Japan was about ready to surrender," he says. "It was just a matter of time. Most of its major cities were destroyed by our bombing, our navy had blockaded the home islands, and the Soviets had just entered the war.

If we had staged a demonstration explosion over Tokyo harbor, we could have convinced the Japanese leadership to surrender without all these casualties."

Rusty listens to his coach with keen interest. He has long been fascinated by the Second World War, having read about it in the books in his father's study and in the school and town libraries. Rusty knows he's not part of this discussion, but he suddenly can't help himself.

"Are you sure about that?" he asks.

Startled, Kirschner turns to Rusty, along with a bunch of other people, including Ms. Levy. He can make out her large eyes in the darkness, and it makes Rusty nervous.

"Well, yes," Kirschner responds, his expression in a puzzled frown, as if to ask, why would I not be?

Rusty says, "Well, up to then we were fighting a brutal war against an enemy that routinely fought to the last man, and each island we captured came at a greater and greater cost in terms of U.S. casualties. You had Japanese civilians commit mass suicides in Saipan, and Kamikaze planes sink a bunch of our ships off Okinawa. We firebombed Tokyo and killed about a hundred thousand people, and nothing happened. And General MacArthur predicted that an invasion of Japan would cost the allies about a million casualties. It seems to me that the bombs may have saved lives in the end."

"The intent was not to save lives," Kirschner counters. "The intent was to wrap up the war before the Soviets could invade Japan. Why do you think we dropped the second bomb on Nagasaki, just three days after Hiroshima?"

"Well, you have a point there," admits Rusty. "Look, I'm not a big fan of nuclear weapons, and I have concerns about nuclear energy in general. I hate that my country actually dropped the bomb on another country. But I have to admit that I have a sort of personal bias toward the bomb."

"A personal bias toward the bomb?" asks Kirschner, again frowning, the lines on his forehead visible in the dim light.

"Well, yes. You see, my dad fought in the Pacific. His ship was sunk by a kamikaze off Okinawa. If we didn't drop the bomb, my dad would have had to participate in the invasion of Japan, which means he wouldn't have gone back to his college when he did, and that means he wouldn't have met my mom, and they wouldn't have had me. So, you see, I owe my very existence to the atom bomb." There is a long uncomfortable silence. "And, um, the University of Illinois, where my parents met." He hears snickering and laughter from the group, including a loud outburst of laughter from Ms. Levy, which startles Rusty. Mr. Kirschner shoulders jerk uncontrollably with his laughter, and the sight makes Rusty laugh as well.

The bus arrives at the high school. Rusty and the others descend from the bus and begin the walk to the locker rooms inside. Just before reaching the door to the building, he feels someone nudge him. It's Ms. Levy.

"Hey Rusty, I really enjoyed listening to you debate with the coach. You're always so quiet. You're a smart kid, you're articulate, you've got a good mind—you should show it off more." She looks at him as if to say, don't you dare disagree with me!

"Um, okay, Ms. Levy, thanks."

She smiles at him and peels away.

Upon entering the boys' locker room, Rusty feels a shove from his left. It's from Larry. "Oooh, Rusty, she thinks you're smart. I bet you have a boner now!"

"Fuck off, Larry," Rusty replies, shoving him back. He could be so fucking juvenile sometimes. Rusty can feel himself blush though, and he *is* getting a hard on. Above all, Rusty feels elation.

NOVEMBER 1978

It's Friday night, and Rusty is enduring yet another harrowing drive with Larry at the wheel, this time to a cinema in Fairfield to see *National Lampoon's Animal House*. Rusty has seen this film once before with his parents, who have recently lifted their restriction on watching R-rated movies. When Larry called him a couple of nights ago to propose seeing the film, Rusty didn't object, for he had loved the movie.

"So, I see you're still out running after school. The fuck's that all about?" asks Larry.

"Shit, I dunno. I guess I wanna stay sharp for indoors," referring to the upcoming winter track season.

"Hey, did I hear right that your girlfriend is gonna be coaching as well?"

"You mean Ms. Levy?"

"Who else would I mean, idiot?" Larry laughs.

"Yeah, I heard something about that," Rusty admits.

He had in fact, heard that Ms. Levy would be the girl's track coach, both for indoor and outdoor. It was certainly a training motivator for Rusty, for he wants to look good now she's going to be around. Both Coaches Kirschner and Scarpella have advised Rusty to keeps the runs at an easy pace though. Once indoor track practices start in December, the harder stuff will begin in earnest.

They pull into the cinema parking lot, and Rusty breathes a sigh of relief. But next comes the anxiety of trying to gain admission. *Animal House* is rated R, meaning that no one under 17 is to be admitted without a parent or adult guardian. Larry is 16, and Rusty is 15. A long line outside the movie house has already formed. The film was released last summer, yet it still draws scores of people who, like Rusty and Larry, have seen it before.

The doors have opened, and now the line begins to move. Rusty's mild anxiety becomes more pronounced; he once did get carded trying to see *Black Sunday,* which bummed him out since he'd read the novel from which the film was based and had loved it. Finally, it's Larry's turn, he pays and gets in. The clerk, a young man not much older than Rusty, gives him a suspicious look, but he accepts Rusty's money and gives him a ticket.

Next, they queue up for snacks. Rusty's usual purchases are a large soda, (usually Pepsi, though he prefers Coke) and a large popcorn. Even at this stage of his life, they seem like guilty pleasures. He knows that this stuff is probably bad for him. For some reason, though, the movie-going experience seems incomplete without junk food.

Rusty and Larry settle into their seats and joke around, occasionally tossing kernels of popcorn at each other. Finally, the film begins. He sees the opening scene where the two hapless freshmen try unsuccessfully to impress the members of the snobby fraternity, before continuing on to the infamous Delta house. They laugh at the scene of them being greeted by John Belushi as he is pissing on the front yard before leading them inside the Delta house.

And it is then that Rusty notices the girl who is bartending at the rush party.

He remembers her as Kate, the girlfriend of Boone, one of the Delta fraternity brothers. This time he can't take his eyes off her whenever she's onscreen. For she has the same shoulder length wavy brown hair, the same large wide-open eyes and the high cheekbones as Ms. Levy. Because of this, Rusty is mesmerized by her, and he looks forward to the scenes where she makes an appearance.

She's not an identical twin of Ms. Levy. Her complexion is paler. The eyes are blue as opposed to Ms. Levy's turquoise. Her nose is smaller. She also appears to have a thinner frame and is not quite as full-figured. Still, Rusty makes a point of looking her up during the final credit sequence. The actress is Karen Allen.

The two leave the theater. Larry jokes about the film, while Rusty dreams on about Ms. Levy and her look-alike actress. They get into Larry's Blazer, and Rusty immediately fastens his seat belt. Larry guns the engine, shoots out of the parking lot, and turns left onto Post Road. This is a problem, because Larry is driving toward Bridgeport, not Westport. Rusty says "Hey, you're going the wrong way."

Larry makes a sudden sharp right turn into a parking lot without slowing down at all. A row of cars sits parked directly in front. Larry swerves his vehicle hard to the right while slamming his brakes. He avoids hitting the parked cars, but he slams hard into a guardrail that serves as a divider between adjacent parking areas.

Like a crash test dummy, Rusty feels his body being thrown forward while simultaneously being restrained by the seat belt. After the loud crash, a profound silence ensues. Rusty sits in shock for a moment and asks himself did this really happen? Rusty turns to Larry, whose forehead is bleeding profusely. His head has struck the steering wheel. Rivulets of blood are running down the bridge of his nose and both of his cheeks. Larry reaches for the ignition and turns the key. The engine struggles, but it's not going to start.

"The fuck are you doing?" asks Rusty, incredulous.

"We gotta get outta here," mumbles Larry.

"Larry, you've wrecked the car, and you've got blood all over your face! You're in no position to drive anywhere." Larry reaches for the ignition again, and Rusty swats his hand away. "Larry, listen to me while I try to save your life. Your fucking head is bleeding!" Larry again reaches for the ignition and Rusty grabs his arm. With his right hand, Rusty seizes the rear-view mirror and angles it toward his friend. "Larry, just look at yourself!" he shouts.

"Oh," Larry mumbles.

"You believe me now. That's a good start." Rusty unbuttons his flannel shirt.

"What are you doing?" Larry asks.

"Gotta do something about that bleeding," replies Rusty. He takes off his flannel and quickly removes his tee shirt. It breaks his heart to do this as the T-shirt is a souvenir from a recent trip to Key West, and it's one of his favorites. He gently applies the shirt to Larry's bloodied face. "Here, can you hold this?" Larry nods his head. Rusty puts his flannel shirt back on. The chilly November air makes going shirtless a bad option. He looks out the windshield and sees a restaurant. "Larry, you think we can make it to that place over there?"

"Yeah," he replies.

Rusty gets out of the car and hurries over to Larry's side. He opens the car door and helps Larry out. Rusty belatedly remembers that he probably should have made sure Larry wasn't hurt anywhere else before having him walk. What if he's broken his legs? It's so hard to do everything right in these sudden situations! Nonetheless, Larry is able to walk with Rusty's assistance.

They enter the restaurant, and an attractive dark-haired hostess gasps.

Rusty says tersely, "Car accident. Need to call an ambulance." She runs off, and a few moments later a middle-aged man appears with some wash cloths. The man tells Rusty that an ambulance is on its way.

"Thanks," Rusty replies. He has one more thing to do, and he's not looking forward to doing it. "By the way, do you have a phone I can use? I need to call my parents. And his."

* * * * *

Rusty sits in his favorite spot in the Northfield High School library, on top of a radiator in a remote corner, reading a book. It's the spot he gravitates to during his free periods, if no one else has taken it. It's especially welcoming during the cold months, when the radiator emits heat, warming the lower posterior. The spot also feels secluded, though the feeling is illusory. To his immediate left is a large window with a view of the courtyard, which serves as a smoking lounge. It's the hangout of the stoners and "play gays," a term for kids into theatre. It is not where the jocks choose to congregate. Also, the hallways bordering the courtyard have large glass windows, so one can see people walking and gathering there.

Libraries have long been Rusty's favorite hangout, particularly since his middle school days. Relentlessly bullied, he had to endure taunts and spitball attacks in classes, but worse treatment awaited him in the hallways, playgrounds, and after school while heading outside to the buses. In those areas, he could expect to be taunted, shoved, tripped, and even sucker punched from behind. He was not a good fighter, and he ended up on the losing end of most battles, so physically defending himself wasn't much of an option. One day, in seventh grade, after being punched in the face in a lunchtime fistfight, Rusty began eating his lunches in the library instead of the cafeteria. It wasn't long before he realized that the one and only place in school where he felt safe was the library. The reason for this was simply because bullies don't hang out in libraries.

But libraries were more than mere oases of safety for Rusty. They were repositories of literature, information and learning. He devoured books on diverse subjects that interested him: sports, military history, music and cinema. He would pore through back issues of magazines and newspapers, reading old articles that would pique his interest. Sometimes, if classroom harassment became too much to bear, he would cut class and head to the library. It was as if his real education was taking place there instead of in the classrooms.

"Rusty!"

Startled, Rusty looks to his right, and there's Ms. Levy, hands on hips, arms akimbo, glaring at him. "Yes, Ms. Levy?"

"I want to talk to you." She looks very angry, and she appears ready to chew him out. What did he do?

"Okay," he responds uneasily.

"I heard you got into a car accident."

"Oh yeah. I guess word has gotten around."

"Well, yeah, when one of our athletes gets hurt and ends up in the hospital, however briefly, it does get around. What were you guys doing?"

Rusty explains truthfully about them seeing *Animal House*. Its not as if they were out doing drugs or getting drunk. Still, the truth does not seem to set Rusty free. She appears appalled.

"Rusty, you could've gotten yourself hurt. I'm really concerned. I've heard a lot about Larry, and believe me, his bad driving is the least of it. I hear he's a real partier, and he's flunking out of school. And you're hanging out with this guy?"

Rusty bristles at that. "He's my best friend, Ms. Levy! I have my reasons."

Ms. Levy appears to backtrack a bit, possibly realizing that she's overstepped. "Look, we all have our reasons for choosing the people we hang out with. I, too, had a close friend in high school who wasn't exactly an upstanding citizen. But I wasn't putting myself in danger by hanging out with her. I just don't want anything bad to happen to you, that's all."

Rusty takes a deep breath, believing the confrontation to be over. "Yeah, well, thank God for seatbelts."

Ms. Levy nods in apparent agreement, then she suddenly changes tack. "So, whatcha reading?"

Rusty displays the book and replies "*Midnight Express* by Billy Hayes."

"Are you reading that for a class?"

Rusty smiles sheepishly and tenses up. Busted again. "Well, no, not really. It's a bad habit, I guess. I tend to read stuff that's not assigned to me."

Ms. Levy doesn't seem at all upset by his reply. In fact, she appears intrigued. "What drew you to that book?"

"Well, I saw the movie just before school started. After the film ended, I talked to this guy who told me he'd read the book, and he said it was excellent. He said it was way different from the movie, and he recommended it to me. Anyway, a couple of days ago I found this copy, right here," he says, pointing to the row of books where it was located. "It is really good. I'm just amazed that a high school library would carry this."

"What else do you like to read?"

Oh my god, she's curious about me! What's this all about? "Um, oh gosh, all kinds of stuff. When I was a kid, my parents wouldn't let me see R-rated movies. So, I read the novels that the movies were based on, like *Marathon Man, Black Sunday* and *One Flew Over the Cuckoo's Nest.* Those books I found on my parents' bookshelf. Next, I went through phases. I'd binge out on certain authors. I went through an S.E. Hinton phase, I went though a Kurt Vonnegut phase."

"Wait, let me guess," Ms. Levy interrupts with a sly smile. "With Vonnegut, you led off with *Breakfast of Champions,* because someone showed you a certain drawing?" She is referring to the crudely drawn image of a clitoris in the text.

Rusty laughs and can feel himself blush. "Yeah, it was pretty funny. But that novel led me to *Slaughterhouse-Five,* which I thought was brilliant."

"You read *Slaughterhouse-Five?*" Her already large eyes open wider.

"Yeah, I did. *Sirens of Titan,* too. Now I'm into novels about the future. I've read *A Clockwork Orange* and *Brave New World.* I'd like to read *1984* sometime. After all, 1984 is what? Only five years away."

"You should read that novel," replies Ms. Levy, her expression serious again. "I worry that we will head in the direction that these dystopian novels are describing."

"What novels?" asks Rusty.

"Dystopian. They describe a bleak future for humanity."

"Oh, okay," says Rusty, hoping he can commit this new word to memory.

"So, Rusty, of all the novels that you've read, is there one that stands out in any way? A novel that surprised you, or made you look at things in a different way?"

Rusty ponders this for a moment. Wow, that is a hell of a question! He hopes that he can come up with an answer for her, preferably an intelligent one. "Hmm. Wait! *Black Sunday!*"

"Really? Why?" asks Ms Levy, appearing surprised.

"Well, you know the plot of the book and movie, right? Crazed ex-POW hijacks a Goodyear blimp and tries to blow up the Super Bowl?"

"Right."

"Well, at one point I found myself feeling sorry for the bad guy. He'd been bullied at school when he was a kid, gotten his head jammed down a toilet, things like that."

"So at least some of the novel was told from the villain's point of view," observes Ms. Levy.

"Yeah, and don't get me wrong. It's not like I was rooting for the bad guy. I just felt some sympathy for him, that's all."

"Who was the author?" she asks.

"Oh, geez. Someone with a real common name. Harris! Thomas Harris."

"He's a pretty good writer," allows Ms. Levy. "I read it, too. It's not my cup of tea, I'm not really into political thrillers, unless it's by Graham Greene or John LeCarre. Still, it's a skill to create a villainous character who's not one-dimensional, whom one can feel a measure of sympathy for. Real life bad guys don't think they're bad guys."

"Not even that Jim Jones guy?" asks Rusty, referring to the leader of a cult who led his followers on what was called a "mass suicide" only a few days earlier.

"I'm sure he had his reasons, Rusty. A congressman was in Guyana investigating him, and he had him killed. He probably sensed that the jig was up, that the world that he had created was about to be destroyed, and he was able to convince everyone else."

"I just don't get it," says Rusty, suddenly indignant. "I mean, 900 people drinking this Kool-Aid that was laced with cyanide,"

"Flavor Aid, Rusty," Ms. Levy corrects him. "They were drinking Flavor Aid."

"Whatever. Didn't anyone there say, 'No, I'm not going to do this. This is absurd, this is wrong.'? No one? Really, sometimes I just don't understand people!"

"I'm glad you feel that way, that you have this moral certitude about it," replies Ms. Levy. "It's important that you not blindly follow leaders, whether they are political or religious. Look at Hitler. He believed that he was going to restore Germany to what he thought was greatness. He was able to convince enough people that he was the man to do it. Look at where that got them. Be very careful with leaders that make these sorts of promises."

Rusty shakes his head at this, trying to both process this information and the fact that he's actually having this conversation with The Ms. Levy. "So, back to *Black Sunday*,'" she says. "You mentioned that you felt sympathy for the villain because he was bullied. Is that something you have personal experience with?"

Rusty doesn't know how to answer this. He wants so badly to impress her and he is terrified of putting her off in any way. The last thing he wants is to make himself vulnerable. But after looking into her eyes and seeing concern and compassion, his defenses crumble.

"Well, yeah," he admits. "Not now, but when I was in middle school. I wasn't popular. I got picked on, called all sorts of names like 'faggot,' and I was beaten up sometimes. You see, I was almost as tall as I am now, but I was twenty pounds lighter, so I was really skinny. I had zits on my face. I didn't do well at school and I got bad grades. I guess I was an easy target. Even girls used to pick on me. But it wasn't just that. Getting bullied is bad, but being shunned is worse. I remember this field trip to Washington, D.C. toward the end of 8th grade. The bus ahead of us broke down. The kids in that bus had to cram into ours. But no one would sit next to me even though it was standing room only. I'll never forget the laughter of the other kids. That's how unpopular I was."

"Oh Rusty, I'm so sorry. I don't see anyone bullying you now, though."

"True. During my first day of school in freshman year, I discovered the weight room next to the boy's gym locker room. I started lifting weights. At first, guys used to kid me, I couldn't even bench a hundred pounds. But I got stronger, and I gained some muscle mass. Not like Arnold Schwarzenegger in *Pumping Iron*, but enough I suppose to make me look like a tougher target. But a few months before that, I found myself a protector."

"Really, who was that?" Ms. Levy asks.

"Well, right after that trip in eighth grade, I met Larry, when I went out for the middle school track team. One day, a bunch of kids confronted me in the hallway. It was pretty similar to the situation you saw me get involved in with Daniel. Larry happened to be nearby. He decked one of them and the others scattered. We've been friends ever since."

Ms. Levy looks quite sad, as if she's about to cry. "Oh God, Rusty!"

"What?"

"I'm so sorry I said what I did about him!"

Rusty suddenly feels bad for Ms. Levy, and he now feels the need to rescue her somehow. "Look, Ms. Levy, he's not a perfect person. He's got problems. His parents are divorced, they fight all the time. He's got a much younger sister with her own problems, and he's got no one to turn to, so he acts out in some really messed up ways. My mom once said that I'm the only stable influence in his life."

Ms. Levy smiles at this. "Well, I'm glad you play that role for him." She looks down at her watch. "I've got to go, another class to teach. I'd like to do this again with you, to talk about novels, running, other things of interest to you."

Rusty is stunned. He can't believe that this beautiful teacher would have any interest in him. "Yes, yes, I'd like that very much, Ms. Levy!" he stammers.

Her smile broadens. "Good. I'll see you." She turns and begins to walk away, but stops suddenly and turns back around, a coy smile forming on her lips. "You know Rusty, if you should be in any of my classes, you'll have to address me as 'Ms. Levy.' And the same is true during track practice. But if you and I are alone like this talking one on one, you can call me 'Carla.'"

"Wow, yes, okay...Carla."

She flashes her broad smile again and walks away a final time.

Carla!

* * * * *

Rusty, his parents and his teammates are in the Cobbs Mill Inn, an upscale restaurant in Northfield, for the cross-country team awards dinner. The restaurant, a former sawmill, is known for being on a river overlooking a large waterfall, and it's indeed a picturesque establishment, the sort of place that would be used for postcards if Northfield were a tourist destination. Until last year, Rusty had never been here. The menu is far too expensive for his father to even consider taking the family to the restaurant. However, it is the go-to place for both the cross-country and track team banquets, so they've been here before.

As Rusty devours his steak, his father turns to him and asks, "Is that Ms. Levi over there?" He gestures to Carla, who is sitting at a table with Coach Kirschner.

His mother, having heard him mispronounce Carla's surname as "Leave-I," laughs.

"Not like the blue jeans, Dad. It's Ms. Lee-Vee, as in Vee-formation," replies Rusty. His father likes to missay names and places in amusing ways—hence his mother's chuckling.

"She's a very pretty girl," observes his dad.

The awards ceremony takes place after dinner. Michael Wiseman receives a trophy for his outstanding service. Coach Kirschner receives an electric golf ball returner; Carla, a tennis racket. The boys and girls each pose for a team photo with their coach for the high school yearbook. After that, there's a few minutes of mingling before it's time to go home.

Rusty stands with his parents, Larry, and Larry's mother, a tall, striking blonde. In her younger days, she was a professional model. Now, she's on the other side of the lens, as a freelance photographer.

Rusty looks around and sees Carla approaching. He smiles and asks, "I see you got yourself a tennis racquet. Do you play?"

"I do," Carla replies. "I've played since I was a girl at summer camp. Sometimes I play with Mrs. Kingsley, if we have a moment and it's nice out, but that's not too often." After a brief pause, she says, "This is a nice place, isn't it? Great place for a wedding rehearsal dinner or reception."

For a moment, Rusty drifts off, imagining his own future wedding reception with Carla. But then he notices Carla casting glances toward his parents. Taking his social cue, Rusty turns and says "Mom, Dad, this is Ms. Levy. She's an English teacher who also coaches the girls."

"Oh, it's a pleasure to meet you!" exclaims his mother.

"Nice to meet you," says his father, smiling appreciatively.

DECEMBER 1978

Rusty and his teammates are sprawled on the cold, hard hallway floor just outside the gym doing stretches on the first day of indoor track practice. Once again, Michael Wiseman is leading the stretching, this time under the watchful eye of Anthony Scarpella, the boys' track coach.

Because Northfield High lacks a field house, the boys' and girls' indoor track teams make do with their surroundings. Runners do their workouts in the hallways, a hazardous undertaking since rounding the corners can result in a head-on collision with an unsuspecting student. The floor surface is unforgiving, and last year Rusty developed a painful case of shin splints that resolved over time. Sometimes if Scarpella has assigned a particularly long workout, Rusty and his fellow runners will run outdoors if the air is not too frigid and the roads are clear of ice.

As tough as it is to run in the hallways, the kids who do field events have their own set of dangers. The pole vaulters, high jumpers, long jumpers and shot putters have to do their workouts in the gym, sharing the space with both the boys' and girls' basketball teams, resulting in high jumpers and pole vaulters being menaced by errant basketballs as they approach the crossbar.

Rusty's track coach, Anthony Scarpella, aka "Tony Scars," has a different personality from Coach Kirschner, to be diplomatic. A rather short yet powerfully built man just shy of fifty, he moves with a catlike agility befitting a man who has kept himself in shape long after his glory days have ended. Mostly bald, with graying hair in the back of his head, he has an eagle-like visage, complete with piercing blue eyes, a large hooked nose, and a scar on his left cheek, the result of a war injury, hence the nickname. Rusty imagines that if Scarpella had pursued an acting career instead of becoming a gym teacher, he'd have been cast as a Roman general.

Unlike Coach Kirschner, Coach Scarpella did not attend an Ivy League university. Scarpella's higher education began in the Marine Corps' notorious boot camp on Parris Island and continued on the battlefields of Korea, where he received his wound, courtesy of a Chinese grenade. After recovering and returning home, he enrolled at Southern Connecticut State College, where he studied physical education and was a star running back on the football team, setting some rushing records that still stood. After college, he got hired as a gym teacher here, eventually becoming the football coach, track coach and finally, athletic director.

Rusty has always gotten along with Scarpella. He's had only had one bad run in with him. The previous spring during the outdoor track season. Rusty had briefly left the track for a warm-up jog before starting his main workout. He was approaching the soccer field where the shot putters, discus and javelin throwers, collectively known as "weightmen," were about to practice. Suddenly he heard someone shouting. He recognized the voice. It was Randy Tarkington, a notoriously ill-tempered and profane groundskeeper who was responsible for the upkeep of all the athletic fields in Northfield. Tarkington had the sort of musculature that only someone on anabolic steroids could possess, and Rusty suspected that he was using them. He had seen Tarkington working out in the high school weight room, bench pressing hundreds of pounds while football players looked on in awe.

As Rusty came closer, he heard Tarkington threaten the athletes with bodily harm if they continued to throw their shots, discuses and javelins. He heard him utter the word "fuck" numerous times, in all its derivations as a noun, verb, and adjective. Finally, he stopped, got into his Ford pickup, and after some squealing of tires was gone, leaving in his wake an acrid smell of burned rubber, some fresh skid marks on School Road, and a group of stunned weightmen.

Rusty jogged over to them. They appeared shell-shocked, unable to utter a syllable. "I saw what happened," said Rusty. It failed to elicit a response. "I think we should tell the coach, don't you?"

After a long pause, one of the throwers managed to mumble "Yeah." "Okay, lets go," replied Rusty.

It was an unlikely sight, a freshman runner, leading a squad of shocked weightmen, some of them seniors. When they arrived at the track, Scarpella immediately spotted Rusty and became visibly angry. "What's goin' on here? Why aren't you doing your workout?"

"Coach, we had an incident on the soccer field just now," replied Rusty. "What happened?"

Rusty gave his account to the coach, while the weightmen behind him silently nodded their heads. It all went well until Rusty said, "He told them 'If you fucking fucks don't get off my fucking soccer field, I'm going to fucking kill you motherfuckers!'"

"Watch your mouth, Rusty!" Scarpella screamed. "Don't give me any of your lip!"

Rusty could feel his blood drain from his skull down to the pit of his stomach, and he began to feel faint. Somehow, he managed to keep his composure. "Coach, those are not my words. I'm merely reporting verbatim what Tarkington said to these guys."

"Oh," responded the coach. Now it was his turn to become pale. Rusty wondered if Scarpella knew the meaning of the word "verbatim." However, Scarpella quickly regained his stride. Jabbing his finger at the weightmen, he yelled "Well, I want you guys to go back down there and continue with your workout!"

"Coach, what about Tarkington?" asked one of the weightmen in a quavering voice.

"You don't worry about Tarkington. I'll take care of him!"

With that, Rusty scampered off to begin his assigned workout. I've done my part here, he thought.

Tarkington never bothered anyone again. He apologized to the weightmen the following day and was not profane from that day forward. Michael Wiseman quipped that Tony Scars must have made him an offer he couldn't refuse. In any event, Rusty began to feel much respect and admiration for his track coach. Scarpella might be a crazed ex-Marine, but if you ran for him, he had your back. No one, not even bodybuilders on steroids, could threaten his athletes and get away with it.

After the calisthenics and stretches are done, Rusty, Larry and the other runners begin their assigned workouts. For Rusty and Larry, it's four 660s and two 330s. Each lap in the hallways is approximately 330 yards, give or take, so it's either two laps or one lap hard with a lap jog in between for recovery.

As they run their laps, Rusty notices Scarpella chatting with Carla. They seem to get along remarkably well, with a certain banter that didn't exist with Mr. Kirschner, and this surprises Rusty. Carla is more of an intellectual, or at least smart as hell, as is Mr. Kirschner. Scarpella will not be confused for an intellectual. And yet, there they are joking with each other like a comic duo.

"Hey Furillo, why don't you pick it up a bit next time," snaps Scarpella. Just as they get beyond earshot, Larry mutters "Hey Coach, why don't you fuck off next time?"

Rusty feels the need to say something. "He means well."

"Yeah, well I wish he'd get off my fucking case," replies Larry.

"He's on your case cuz you're both talented and lazy, and that drives him nuts. Hell, it drives me nuts. If I was as talented as you, I'd be kicking Trevor Levelle's ass."

The runner that Rusty is referring to is a fellow sophomore who competes for New Milford High School. As a freshman he has already set records and won the Western Connecticut Conference (WCC) Championships in both indoor and outdoor track. Unfortunately, Lavelle competes in the same events as Rusty, which dispirits him, since there is no way Rusty will win a league title as long at Lavelle is in the running.

They come to the end of their recovery lap, and Rusty remembers that they have just finished the penultimate or second-to-last 660. He's remembering that word from a vocabulary assignment from some time ago, and it has turned out to be an easy word to remember, since the penultimate repeat of any workout is always harder than the last one, at least mentally, anyway, because you know that you still have one more to go.

"Okay, Larry, last one to go. Ready to make Tony Scars happy?"

"Fuck you," replies Larry.

"I'll take that as a yes. Three, two, one, go."

Off they run. They sprint past the cafeteria and faculty offices, take a left and run past the smoking lounge, dodging stoners along the way, take another left and run past the auditorium, front door entrance and library, take another left just before the entrance of the gym, run the final stretch to where they started before beginning their second lap. As they run the final lap, they cruise past female runners and slower boys. They come to the final stretch where Carla and Scarpella are waiting. Larry surges ahead but Rusty stays close, he wants it to look good for the both of them. When they finish, Scarpella says "Good job, Larry, that was better."

"Nice run, Rusty," says Carla.

Rusty smiles and says, "Thank you," to Carla. Turning to Larry he says, "That wasn't so bad, was it?"

* * * * *

Rusty and Larry are out bowling at Westport Lanes, a large bowling alley in Westport, a town just south of Northfield. It's a much larger community, and unlike Northfield, it actually offers diversions, including two movie theatres, a 24-hour diner, and a town beach in the summer. During daytime hours Main Street is a wonderful place to browse and shop, with two bookstores and Klein's, a department store that also has a good record section where Rusty buys his rock albums. For those 18 and older, there are nightclubs like Backstage and Club 300.

The bowling alley is a place where Rusty and Larry go frequently because Larry happens to be good at the sport. Rusty admires and envies Larry's power and form as he launches the sixteen-pound balls down the alley, frequently knocking down all ten pins in the frame for a strike.

Rusty has never gotten the hang of bowling. The whole process feels weird, beginning when exchanging his comfortable sneakers for a set of ill-fitting bowling shoes. The balls feel heavy and awkward in his hands, and even with lighter ones, he has difficulty controlling the ball, resulting in frequent gutter balls. Larry regularly scores over 200 points a game, but for Rusty, scoring over 100 is a good result. Still, despite these challenges and drawbacks, Rusty manages to enjoy himself. Living in a town with scant diversions makes any one of them desirable.

They have just finished a game when Larry asks "Wanna play one more?"

They go to the front desk to pay for another sheet to keep track of their scores. This time, Rusty is having a better go of it. His balls aren't ending up in the gutter, instead traveling straight down the lane, occasionally even knocking all ten pins down. He's not sure what he's doing right this time. He still loses to Larry, who scores 205. Still, Rusty's 172 is unprecedented. At least I gave Larry a decent game, he thinks.

They saunter back to the front desk to turn in the bowling shoes and retrieve their sneakers. Larry asks, "What should we do now?"

"I dunno. Head home?"

"Nah, I don't feel like dealing with my mom just yet. I'm kinda hungry. Let's go to the diner."

"Yeah, okay."

Rusty and Larry have occasionally gone to the Sherwood Diner. It's a relatively safe place to dine; a nearby Dairy Queen is a big hangout for Westport jocks, and kids from other towns have gotten harassed. The diner draws an interesting after-hours crowd of patrons from a next-door strip club and a nearby gay bar who descend on the place around closing time. It is also across the street from a state trooper's barracks, so it's a cop hangout as well.

They are driving in a new Chevy Blazer that Larry's rich dad got him after the accident. Larry's driving hasn't changed a bit. They speed down Post Road before pulling into the parking lot.

They enter the diner and Rusty sees that the place is about three-quarters full. Most of the patrons are teens like himself, and there's a smattering of adults. It's just after midnight: in about an hour, when the nearby bars close, it will be completely packed. As they walk toward an empty booth, Rusty notices a group of boys glaring at him. They are wearing the black and white varsity jackets of the local high school here. Rusty averts his eyes and sits with Larry.

A waitress offers them a menu, but they both know what they want, a hamburger with French fries and cole slaw and a Coke. After she leaves, Larry asks "So Raz, have you banged the teacher yet?"

"Christ, Larry, don't be so fucking gross. Of course there's nothing going on between us, and there never will be. If I'm lucky, we talk about literature or whatever." He glances to his left to find the Westport gang is still glaring at him.

"I hear there's a dance at the gym next Saturday. Maybe she'll be there."

"Hey Larry, not to change the subject, but what's going on with you and your mom?"

"Eh, she's just on my case about a lot of shit."

"Such as what?"

"My grades, for one thing"

"How are they?"

"What do you think?"

"Anything else going on?" asks Rusty.

"My mom's got a new boyfriend."

"Really? You've met him?"

"Yeah, he's a Black guy, and I think he's a lot younger than she is."

"That bother you?" asks Rusty.

"I don't know." Larry shrugs. "My dad's had a girlfriend for a while, and she don't look much older than me."

The waitress arrives with their order. As she places the food on the table, Rusty again glances to his left, then leans forward. He says in a voice just above a whisper, "There's a bunch of guys giving me the skunk eye. Don't look obvious. Just look over on your right, three o'clock."

Larry glances over, and his face hardens. "Fuckin' Staples douchebags." Staples is the name of the local high school.

Occasionally, Rusty and Larry glance over to these local jocks, who continue to glower at them. C'mon guys, Rusty thinks, just finish your meal and get the fuck out. We have no quarrel with you. After a while, the group gets up and leaves. Rusty breathes a sigh of relief and is now able to enjoy his hamburger and fries.

About twenty minutes later, Rusty and Larry leave a tip on the table and head to the cashier to settle up. They leave the diner and step into the parking lot when he hears "Hey, faggot!"

Rusty and Larry turn and see the group of jocks glowering at him. "Who are you calling a faggot?" retorts Larry.

"I'm talking to you, numbnuts! You faggots just came from The Brooke, didn't you?" The lead thug is referring to The Brooke Café, a gay bar that's two buildings away from the diner. It's a somewhat strange accusation, since both Rusty and Larry are too young to be admitted there, even if they were inclined to go. Rusty suspects that attempting to explain this fact would be futile. He also notices that there are six of these guys, versus him and Larry. He is thinking of possible ways to defuse this situation when Larry says, "Why don't you go fuck your mother!"

Okay, de-escalation isn't happening. Enraged, the leader of the pack lunges at Larry. The two grapple, then fall to the pavement, the leader on top of Larry, cocking his fist to punch him out. Without thinking, Rusty charges forward, plowing into him and knocking him off Larry. Sprawled on the pavement, Rusty knows that this was a bad move, since the rest of them are now going to kick the shit out of him. Sure enough, he feels a large set of hands gripping each of his shoulders.

Rusty is lifted skyward, his feet clear off the ground. Who the fuck is attacking me, King Kong? Rusty is expecting to get slammed, either on the pavement or on the hood of a car. Instead, the set of hands gently place him back on his feet, and he is let go. Rusty whirls around and finds himself facing a cop, who is possibly the largest human being he has ever seen in person. Jabbing an index finger at Rusty he snarls "Get out!"

"Okay, bye!" Rusty turns and runs toward Larry's vehicle. Reaching it, he stops and turns, looking for Larry.

There he is. "Get in the car!" Larry yells.

The two pile inside and slam the doors shut. Gasping, Rusty says "Holy shit, we are so lucky we weren't busted or beaten up. How the hell is it that we weren't arrested?"

"I don't know, let's just get the fuck out of here." Larry starts the ignition.

"Whoa, Larry, before we go, just one thing."

"What?"

"Let's drive just a little slower going home, okay? I don't want to die tonight."

* * * * *

The following weekend, Rusty is attending the Christmas dance at the high school gym. He has never attended a school dance before, and now he sees he hasn't been missing much. There is scant interaction between boys and girls. The boys are off to the side staring sullenly at the girls, who hang out in the center of the gym dancing or chatting amongst themselves, though conversation is difficult above the music. The most interesting thing about the event is the band itself, which is pretty good. Rusty watches the musicians as they play up-tempo numbers in a futile attempt to get people dancing. After a while, even the music is not enough, and Rusty decides to walk around.

He leaves the gym and enters the hallway where the coats and jackets are stored. Thinking that he might pick up his down jacket before calling his parents for a ride home, he stops short, for he sees Carla sitting at the table, reading a book. He stands there, staring at her, until she looks up.

He asks, "They got you working as a coat check girl?"

Carla laughs. "Yes, Rusty, it appears I am. How are you?"

Rusty shrugs. "Okay, I guess. What are you reading?"

Carla shows him the cover for *The Sea, The Sea*. "It's by Iris Murdoch. I like her novels. She writes about intelligent and erudite people who fall for the wrong person." She gestures at a nearby chair. "Take a seat, keep me company."

"Sure!" Rusty takes the chair and sits down.

"Where's Larry?" Carla asks.

"He's with his dad this weekend."

"I noticed that his left eye looked bruised this week. Did he get into a fight?

"Well, yeah, he kind of did. Actually, we both did."

"What?" yelps Carla. Rusty tells her about the incident at the diner after they went bowling. As expected, Carla looks appalled.

"Look, Carla, I know you're not crazy about Larry."

"No, Rusty, it's not that. I'm upset that you and Larry were targeted because they thought you were gay."

"But we're not gay."

"That's not the point, Rusty. They thought you were, and that's why they stalked and attacked you. I have friends who are gay back home in the city. My best friend from high school is a lesbian. They are wonderful people, just like you and me except that their desires differ from ours. You know, Rusty, a lot of them are great artists. If you like reading Oscar Wilde, or if you like the music of Elton John or The Village People, then maybe you should give these people a little more respect."

Feeling chastened even though he hasn't said anything derogatory about gay people, Rusty looks down. "Actually, I do feel a lot of respect for them now. I mean, we weren't doing anything wrong, we were just having a hamburger and a coke. To be attacked just for being who you are or what they think you are, and to have to live with that threat all your life, that's so messed up."

"It is messed up, and I'm glad you see it that way. It's not just gays who experience this. Look at what Black people have gone through, Latinos, and other minorities. And we Jews are no strangers to hate."

"Yeah, that's right."

"So, lets talk about something else. What else is going on with you?"

"Hmm..." Rusty ponders. "Well, my birthday's coming up."

"Oh, happy birthday! And how old are you now?"

"I turn sixteen on Wednesday." God, why can't I be older?

"Really?" Carla says, her eyes wide open.

She seems unusually happy to be hearing this. Why?

She asks, "Looking forward to being able to drive a car?"

"Oh God, yes!"

Suddenly, another voice says, "Okay Carla, your shift's over." It's Mrs. Kingsley the attractive blond gym teacher who's Carla's friend at work.

"Thanks, Marsha!" Turning back to Rusty, she says "Well, I'm headed home, but before I go, do you want to dance a little bit?"

Rusty feels a shock to his system. Do I want to dance a little bit? "Um, sure!"

Rusty follows Carla as they walk back to the gym. The band has just started playing "Call Me the Breeze," a song popularized by Lynyrd Skynyrd. This time, some kids of both genders are on the dance floor, and Rusty and Carla join them. It's just freestyle dancing and Rusty would much rather do a slow dance with her, but that's not realistic at a school dance. Still, Rusty enjoys watching Carla shimmy to the beat. Rusty feels a little self-conscious dancing with a teacher in front of other kids, and he doesn't dare look at anyone other than Carla. He thinks about Carla's reaction when he told her he was about to turn sixteen, and then he remembers that conversation at the beginning of the school year, when Michael Wiseman said that the age of consent was sixteen. Oh my god, in a few days, she'll be legally able to have sex with me! When the song ends Carla says, "Thank you Rusty, that was nice. I'm going to head home."

"Can I walk you to your car?" Oh god, did I just ask her that?

Carla seems surprised, but not unpleasantly so. "Sure, thank you."

Carla gathers her coat, and they leave the building together. As they walk toward the school parking lot she says, "You know, about what we talked about earlier, I am worried about you being with Larry. This is the second time I've heard about a dangerous situation where you could have gotten hurt. You guys are so lucky that the cops were there."

"Yeah, I know."

They reach the parking lot. "Well, this is my car. Thank you for walking me."

"Sure, no problem."

She turns and faces Rusty, a worried look etched on her moonlit face. "Promise me you'll be careful with Larry?"

"Yeah, sure, Carla, I promise."

"Good." She gently touches his arm. It's a platonic gesture, but it excites Rusty. Staring intently at Rusty she says, "I care about you."

Rusty stands shivering in the dark as Carla gets into her car and drives away. He again thinks about the happy implications of his upcoming birthday.

"I care about you." She actually said that.

1979

JANUARY 1979

Kevin Malinowski is Rusty's lab partner in chemistry class. A fellow sophomore, he's a new kid, having just moved here with his family from some small town in Pennsylvania. He's tall, close to Rusty's height, with brown hair, and he has an easygoing friendliness that one associates with someone from a rural background. He has certainly done well socially, even managing to win the heart of Danielle Fournier, a gorgeous brunette who bears a striking resemblance to the actress Jacqueline Smith, a star of *Charlie's Angels*. She's in her junior year and on the cheerleading team. Rusty doesn't know much else about him. He's just someone he's been with while fumbling about with test tubes, beakers and Bunsen burners.

All this changes one day toward the end of indoor track practice. Rusty and Larry have finished the main part of their workout and are jogging a couple of cooldown laps when they hear music that sounds almost foreign to Rusty. He slows to a stop. "You hear that?"

Larry, also stopping says "Yeah, what the fuck is that?"

"Sounds like a banjo, don't it."

"Yeah, squeal like a pig music," snorts Larry.

Puzzled and intrigued by the twangy sound, Rusty says, "Let's check this out." They jog over to the source of the sound, and there is Kevin, playing his instrument, with Danielle standing there looking lovestruck. The music he's playing is bluegrass, the genre of music now associated with the film *Deliverance,* and its infamous forced sodomy scene, which Larry was referring to. This is unfortunate, Rusty realizes, because he likes the music that Kevin's playing. Kevin's a pretty good banjo picker. Rusty notices that the song he's playing is in three chords, and after a couple of repititions, he knows the chord progression. This gives him an idea.

Kevin finishes his song. Rusty claps his hands, surprising both Kevin and Danielle. "Wow, all these months together in chem lab and I didn't know this about you. I happen to play guitar myself."

"Really?" Kevin looks genuinely surprised.

"Yeah, we have the same free period tomorrow, right? How about I bring my guitar and we jam together?"

"That sounds great!"

The two continue their jog. Larry asks, "Have you ever played this kind of music before?"

"Nope."

"And you're gonna jam with this kid in school in front of everyone?

"I guess."

"You're fucking nuts," says Larry.

"Maybe."

The next day, Rusty meets Kevin in the smoking lounge area, after Rusty had hurriedly retrieved his guitar from a remote corner in the backstage area of the auditorium, which is currently in use by the high school orchestra. They both decided on the smoking lounge, since the stoners would probably be a more receptive audience than the jocks. Outside, its cold and rainy, which it has been all month, so they'll have to play in the hallway. Not perfect, but it'll have to do.

Kevin starts off a song. Just as Rusty had suspected and hoped, he is able to get the progression very quickly, though Kevin helpfully nods his head to cue Rusty on the chord changes. A dozen or so denim-clad, shaggy-haired stoner kids gather around, appearing astounded the way Rusty was, that anyone would be playing bluegrass here in Northfield, Connecticut. Suddenly, the crowd of kids parts to make way for someone, and Carla appears. Rusty now feels very nervous: his skin becomes clammy, and his heart is racing, as he tries desperately not to be distracted, so that he can follow Kevin's lead. Finally, the song ends. Rusty takes a deep breath. Carla claps enthusiastically.

"Rusty, you bum! You never told me you played guitar!"

"Well, yeah...I do," says Rusty, feeling himself blush.

"Well, I shouldn't scold you too much. I never told you that I play and sing as well."

"Really?"

"You want to play us a song?" asks Kevin.

"Sure!" says Carla.

Astonished, Rusty hands her his guitar and pick. Once the guitar strap is on her shoulder, she strums a couple of chords to get the feel of the instrument before she starts her song.

The song she plays is country influenced, surprising Rusty, since

Brooklyn probably isn't a hotbed of country music. It's a song of yearning, about the love a girl has for a boy she can't be with. Carla's guitar playing is only so-so, but her mezzo-soprano voice is exquisite, perfectly conveying the emotion.

When Carla finishes, Rusty and many other students applaud. Rusty says "That's a great song! Who wrote it?"

Carla smiles and blushes. "Actually, I wrote it."

"You're a songwriter?"

"Well, I've written a few songs, but that doesn't make me a songwriter. I've written poetry, including some sonnets, but that doesn't make me a poet, either. What I really want to do is write novels."

"Wow, I didn't know that! Have you written one yet?"

"I'm working on it," she replies with a smile. She hands the guitar and pick back to Rusty. "You were great, Rusty. You should play for me sometime."

Rusty watches her as she walks off. A novelist, poet, musician, singer and a songwriter, and she's gorgeous. What a goddess! A real-life renaissance woman. He turns and sees Kevin grinning at him. "What?" Rusty asks.

Kevin doesn't answer. Instead, he slowly shakes his head.

"What?" Rusty asks again.

"Earth to Rusty! Ground control to Major Rusty!"

"What?" Rusty nearly shouts.

"That teacher wants to marry you, that's what."

* * * * *

The following day, Rusty is at his locker, throwing in his notebook for English, and taking out his chemistry textbook and notebook. He slams his locker shut, turns, and sees Carla standing right in front of him, blocking his way. Startled, he says, "Um, Carla, I mean Ms. Levy, hi!"

"Rusty, I just wanted to chat with you. I heard that there's going to be a talent show in a couple of weeks."

"Okay, what about it?"

"I think you should be in it."

"What?"

"I think you should perform in it. You were so good with that other kid."

"With Kevin, you mean?"

"Yes, yes," she answers impatiently. "I want you to sign up. I think it will be good for you." She casts him the same wide-eyed glare she did back in October, when she encouraged him to be more talkative. The don't-you-dare-say-no-to-me kind of look, Rusty thinks. Carla says, "I'm going to be in it too, by the way!"

"What? Really?"

"Yes, it's open to faculty as well as the students. Will that influence your decision?" she asks, her eyebrows rising.

"Okay, okay, let me talk to Kevin and see what he says. There's no way I'm doing this alone. I am not a solo performer." Rusty remembers Kevin's in his next class.

"Good! Promise me that you'll talk to him?"

"Yes, Ms. Levy!"

A half hour later, Rusty and Kevin are in chemistry lab. Kevin is lighting a Bunsen burner when Rusty asks, "You've heard of this talent show that's happening next month?"

"Yeah," replies Kevin, having just ignited the burner. "Why?"

"Uh, someone suggested we might be a good act."

Kevin's eyebrows rise, and a sly smile crosses his face. "And who might that person be? Could it be that certain teacher who has eyes for you?"

Rusty laughs sheepishly and feels himself blush. "Oh god. If only that were true. But, yeah, it's her. Look, if you don't want to do it, that's cool. I just thought..."

"Well actually, I was thinking of asking you, but you beat me to it," interrupts Kevin. "Give me your notebook." Rusty shoves it to Kevin, who opens it and jots down his phone number on a corner of a page. "We should get together and jam, find a couple of songs that we do well, and rehearse the hell out of them. I have a couple of other kids in mind who can round us out. Agree?"

"Yeah, sure," replies Rusty. *Other kids too? Oh, fuck.*

* * * * *

Rusty arrives at Kevin's house on a Saturday afternoon, after having been dropped off by his mom. He walks toward the front door of yet another colonial house, tightly gripping the handle of his guitar case. He rings the doorbell, and within seconds Kevin appears. "Hey, come on in," he says.

Rusty follows Kevin inside to the den where he sees two stoners, a boy and a girl. The sight of the girl startles Rusty. "You guys know each other?" asks Kevin.

"You're Tim, right?" asks Rusty, correctly guessing the first name of Tim Spitz, a junior who is cradling an upright bass.

"Yup," he replies.

"Hi Rusty!" says the girl with a smile. Laura Davis, a fellow sophomore, is a girl Rusty has known since middle school, and whom he had a crush on in eighth and ninth grade. She's an attractive girl, with long dark brown hair, matching dark eyes and a Rubenesque figure. She has a reputation as a partier and for sleeping around. In the 8th grade, she was hospitalized after drinking booze and Nyquil at a middle school dance. Despite all that, she somehow manages to make the honor roll every quarter.

"How's it goin'?" Rusty asks. "I didn't know you played violin."

"I didn't know you played guitar!"

"Yeah, I've been taking lessons for a while. I was jamming with Kevin one day, and Ms. Levy happened to walk by. The next day, she cornered me and insisted that I do the talent show."

"Ms. Levy? I have her for English. I love her!"

"Really?" replies Rusty, suddenly very interested in what Laura has to say.

"She's a wonderful teacher, Rusty. She knows how to get the best out of all her students. I'm not at all surprised that she talked you into this."

Kevin looks at Rusty with a sly and knowing smile. "Okay, you guys, ready to get started? I have some songs that are possibilities, we're only playing two at the show, so its just a matter of finding a couple that we're solid on."

Rusty puts down his guitar case, opens it and takes out his instrument. My first time playing with other people except Kevin, he thinks.

FEBRUARY 1979

Rusty and his new bandmates await their cue backstage during the "It's Saturday Night!" talent show at the Northfield High School auditorium. The event is modeled on the popular *Saturday Night Live* TV show, with comedy skits mixed in with musical acts. There are scores of people in attendance: students, parents, and a few faculty members, including Carla, who will be performing later. Rusty is in a state of abject terror. He has never performed publicly in any way before, and knowing that he's part of a group, and that Kevin will be handling the vocals as well as most of the instrumental leads does not seem to assuage his fear. The band has rehearsed twice at Kevin's house, and both times he has left with a profound respect for his new bandmates, and a feeling that he's quite inferior to them. The last time he felt this scared was when a tornado tore through his neighborhood in Illinois, when he was four. *Jesus, it's no wonder musicians do drugs!*

"Psst! Hey Rusty!" He hears a loudly whispered voice behind him. Rusty turns around and sees Larry beckoning him over.

"What's up, Larry?" Rusty asks impatiently.

"Ready to become a rock star?"

"Fuck no!"

"Why not?"

"I'm scared shitless, that's why. I mean, look at all these people out there!"

"I got something that might help," Larry says.

"What's that?"

Larry opens his down jacket and takes out a bottle. Rusty looks at the label, which reads "Southern Comfort".

"Let's go to a better place," Larry suggests. They find a dark corner of the back-stage area. Rusty takes the bottle, brings it to his mouth and takes a tentative sip. Realizing that he can tolerate it, he takes a bigger swallow. The effect is instantaneous. He feels his jangly nerves become calm. He's still nervous, but now it feels manageable. He takes one more swallow and returns the bottle to Larry.

"Thanks."

An upperclassman is on stage, doing a decent impression of the comic Steve Martin. Mr. Estabrook, a music teacher who is serving as stage manager and emcee, says to Rusty and Kevin, "Okay guys, you're on in a couple of minutes." The four kids stand just outside stage left as the upperclassman continues to perform. Finally, he's finished, the audience applauds, and he leaves the stage. Mr. Estabrook enters and makes his intro, and Rusty steps into the abyss.

Fifteen minutes later, Rusty stands in the backstage area feeling relieved and ecstatic. Relieved because it's over, ecstatic that it has gone over well. It was not a perfect performance on Rusty's part—he made a couple of mistakes with chord changes, but no one seems to have noticed. A number of students and adults have remarked on how original their act was, since one doesn't hear much country and bluegrass music here in Connecticut.

A group of students are onstage performing a "Weekend Update" skit. Carla is standing by, waiting her turn to perform. She wears a black sweater and a tan, mid-length skirt, and she holds an electric guitar, which is strapped around her upper back. The skit finishes, and Mr. Estabrook goes on stage to introduce Carla, who receives much applause. She really has become popular, Rusty realizes. With confidence, she strides onto the stage, plugs her guitar into a small amp, adjusts the mic stand, and strums a few chords to make sure it's still in tune. Smiling, she says, "I'm going to perform for you a song written by someone I've loved and worshiped since I was a girl in high school. Her name is Joni Mitchell."

Carla kicks off the song, and once she starts singing, Rusty recognizes it: "California." He recalls his sister Patti playing the album *Blue*, over and over again, when she was home on college break. Rusty even remembers that "California" is the first song on Side Two.

It is one thing to physically desire someone, or even to be infatuated with that person. It is another thing to be in thrall. Rusty stands transfixed as the overhead spotlights give Carla's wavy brown hair a newfound glow. Softly strumming her guitar, she sings with an ache and passion that rivals Joni's original version. At one point in the song, she hits a high note and holds it for several long seconds, causing spontaneous cheering and applause from the audience. Laura Davis, the stoner girl who Rusty had not long ago fancied from afar, sidles up to him and asks, "Isn't she amazing?"

Rusty doesn't even turn to face her, because he can't take his eyes off

Carla. Staring at Carla, he nods his head and says "Yeah, I'm speechless." Some moments are just too beautiful for words.

When Carla finishes her song, she has to wait a few moments for the applause to die down. When it does, she says "Thank you. Next, I'm going to perform a song that I wrote called 'About a Boy.'" When Carla kicks off that song, Rusty recognizes it as the song that she played in the hallway last month.

An hour later, Rusty is standing in the auditorium with his parents, Kevin's parents and Danielle, Kevin's adoring cheerleader girlfriend. Rusty looks around as Kevin talks with everyone. There is that one person he really wants to see, and here she comes. Carla is approaching, with a big smile. When she gets to him, she says to everyone, "You guys were great!" She turns to Rusty and says "I'm so proud of you. I knew you were reluctant at first, but I also knew this would be great for your self -confidence. And am I right?"

"Yes, Carla, you are. I feel great about tonight."

"Good," she says, still smiling.

"By the way you, too, were magnificent. You should make a record, particularly if you have an original tune."

Carla blushes. "Well, maybe if my ambitions for writing the great American novel don't pan out."

"So, why 'California?' Do you want to move there?" Rusty asks.

"Oh, god no," replies Carla. "I just love the song, that's all. I love how she writes about the connection and longing that she feels for her home, even if she's been traveling to wonderful exotic places. It's how I feel about New York City, I guess."

The two rejoin Kevin and the others. Kevin nudges Rusty.

* * * * *

Rusty sits in the cafeteria during lunch break, finishing a peanut butter and jelly sandwich, before moving on to a banana. Unlike many other kids, Rusty never buys his lunches at the cafeteria. Instead, his mother lovingly packs his lunch in a brown paper bag. As for company, he occasionally eats with others, but usually he eats alone, a carryover from his middle school days when he had no friends. This time, though, Larry has just gotten his food, and is carrying his tray over to where Rusty is.

"Hey, rock star," Larry says.

Rusty laughs. "What's up?"

"Greg Johnson's just come down with mono." He takes a seat opposite Rusty.

"That sucks."

"Yeah, he was supposed to go with us to a rock concert Saturday. That shit ain't happening."

"Wow, damn," says Rusty sympathetically.

"Anyway, that means his ticket is available. Think you want to come?"

"Who's playing?"

"Outlaws, and some group named Molly Hatchet is opening."

"Huh," says Rusty. He's heard of Outlaws (for some reason, there's no "The" before "Outlaws"), though he's much more familiar with the work of other Southern rock bands like Lynyrd Skynyrd, The Allman Brothers, and The Marshall Tucker Band, who are three of his favorite acts. "How much is the ticket?" he asks.

"$6.50"

"Where are they playing?"

"New Haven Coliseum," says Larry.

"I can swing that," Rusty replies. "Not sure if my folks will let me go, but I'm interested."

* * * * *

Two nights later, Rusty sits in a van with four other boys including Larry, on their way to New Haven Coliseum. The other three, Paul Anderson who is driving his dad's van, Barry Meyerson, and Ray Cunningham, are kids Rusty has known since grade school, but until now have not really come into his social orbit. They have all pitched in and have managed to procure a case of beer and a bottle of Bacardi 151. The drinking age in Connecticut is 18, and Paul, the oldest of the five, is only 17. However, a couple of the kids have fake IDs. Rusty is nursing a can of Budweiser. At 16, his experience with alcohol is limited, and he's not crazy about the taste of beer. Perhaps it's an acquired taste as one reaches adulthood, he reasons. Rusty certainly likes the effect that it has on him though. He feels much more relaxed with the kids who are with him, and he hasn't forgotten about how those sips of Southern Comfort helped him overcome his stage fright at the talent show. He thinks, now I understand why they call it "liquid courage."

Next, the bottle of Bacardi 151 is being passed around. There's something menacing about that bottle, Rusty thinks, as it gets nearer. Maybe it's the way the others grimace as they take a hit. Finally, the bottle is passed to him. Rusty takes the bottle with trepidation, brings it to his lips and attempts a swallow.

Immediately, Rusty gags and begins to cough. It feels like his throat was doused with gasoline and set aflame.

Laughter erupts from the others. "Lightweight," jeers one the kids.

"Wimp!" yells another.

"Christ, how can anybody drink this shit?" gasps Rusty passing the bottle to Larry, who calmly takes the bottle and takes several swallows. "Whoa Larry, take it easy!" Rusty says.

"I've got a stomach of steel," says Larry dismissively before handing off the bottle.

The ride to New Haven takes another half hour. Each time the bottle is passed to Rusty, he gingerly brings it to his lips and takes the smallest of sips. Even that is difficult to swallow down. This Bacardi shit is like lighter fluid, he thinks. After several go arounds, Larry polishes off the bottle.

They arrive in the city and soon find the Coliseum. Now they are inching along on a long ramp leading to the parking area. "Good thing we allowed ourselves time to get here," says Barry, a homeroom classmate of Rusty's back in seventh grade.

"Why's that?" asks Rusty.

"Parking here sucks. The parking lot is actually on top of the arena. We have to crawl through this long ramp just to get to it."

"Why is it on top?"

"Something about the high-water tables here in New Haven, they couldn't build it below," explains Barry before finishing off his can of beer. As the van inches along, Rusty notices that Larry has become uncharacteristically quiet. This concerns him.

After about another twenty minutes the van reaches the parking area. Once the van is parked, the boys pile out. The booze has worked its way through their bodies, and they now need to find the men's room before taking their seats in the arena.

This is Rusty's first rock concert, so he doesn't know what to expect. Once he shows his ticket he is admitted to the arena, which is full of people.

It appears to be a sold-out show. The stage is empty, but several electric guitars are propped up on stands. Behind them looms a mountainous drum kit perched on a riser—easily the largest drum kit he has ever seen. The collective stench of marijuana smoke exhaled from the lungs of hundreds of concertgoers fills the air, and Rusty feels somewhat short of breath. He turns to Larry, who is silent and slack-jawed. He wonders if Larry is as awestruck as he is or that maybe he had a bit too much of that Bacardi 151 after all. In the row directly in front is a young couple, a dark-haired boy and a blond girl, who look not much older than Rusty. They are arm in arm, occasionally kissing each other, and obviously very much in love. Rusty imagines himself being with Carla like this at a future rock concert, and the thought takes his mind off the lack of breathable air.

Suddenly, a group of young men enter the stage, and the crowd erupts. Many of them have exceptionally long hair, far past their shoulder blades. The lead singer is a rather heavyset man, unlike the others, who are rail thin, and he wears a red T- shirt that reads "Redneck Power" in white letters.

The band kicks off its first song, an up-tempo number obviously designed to get the crowd revved up. Molly Hatchet is a six-piece band with three guitarists, a not uncommon arrangement in southern rock bands. The three each perform blistering solos at various points in the song, effortlessly throwing out dozens of notes per measure. How the fuck do they do that, Rusty wonders. The lead vocalist, who does not play an instrument, sings in a distinctive raspy growl. It is not the prettiest of voices, but it perfectly matches the music. These guys are good, they really have the chops, Rusty thinks. If they don't hit the big time, then there's something very wrong in the music world.

Once the band has finished the first song, Rusty turns to Larry. He is still silent and slack jawed, but now his eyes are glazed over, and his face has turned to various shades of gray and green. "Larry, are you okay?" Rusty yells. There is no response from Larry, except his mouth has opened a tad wider. "Larry, are you okay?" Rusty asks again, trying to make himself heard above the din of the crowd.

Suddenly a stream of yellowish liquid shoots out of Larry's mouth with such force that it travels in a straight line for about a yard before arcing downward and dispersing, soaking the couple in front of them. The girl screams in horror. Her boyfriend stands shocked and uncomprehending for a moment before looking at Larry. Realizing what has happened, a look of rage crosses his face, and he attempts to climb over his seat and attack Larry. Yelling "Whoa-whoa-whoa!" Rusty raises his hands to fend off an attack that never comes because a swarm of alert security guys has seized Larry and yanked him away, while others are restraining the enraged boyfriend. Rusty watches helplessly as they drag Larry away. "Aw fuck, where are they taking him?" asks Rusty.

"They're just throwing him out. He'll be all right," says Paul. "He's fucked up. Rusty, don't worry about it."

But he does worry about it. After Molly Hatchett's set ends, he excuses himself to look around, but he does not find Larry. He goes back inside to the concert.

More than two hours later after the concert ends, Rusty and the others leave the arena. The talk is of the highlights of the concert, as well as the obvious low point. Rusty remains quiet. "Worried about Larry?" asks Barry.

"Yeah," replies Rusty.

"He probably didn't get very far, he might still be in the garage somewhere."

Rusty hopes he's right. He wonders why they felt compelled to buy that damned bottle of Bacardi 151. A bottle of Southern Comfort would have sufficed. It's easier to drink and it would have been a much more appropriate spirit for an evening of southern rock.

They reach the van and Paul digs into his pocket for the keys. "Shhh!" hisses Barry. "I hear something."

Rusty and the others cock their heads and listen. There's a lot of background noise to filter with people talking as they walk to their vehicles, car engines starting, and cars beginning to drive off. But soon Rusty hears a faint moaning in the distance. "Rusty...Rusty!"

"He's down there!" Rusty shouts, pointing his finger in the direction of the sound. He takes off running, the others pursuing him, and as he runs, he hears Larry's voice grow louder. Soon he finds him. He is standing, but barely, his body lurched against the concrete wall of the garage. "Rusty!" he cries out again.

"I'm here, Larry, I got you," says Rusty, seizing his friend. The other kids catch up. "You think you can walk with us to the van?" Rusty asks. Larry attempts to step forward, but soon sinks to his knees. "I think we better get the van down here." Paul turns and runs back up toward the van.

It takes two guys, Rusty and Barry, to help Larry into the van. Minutes after leaving the coliseum, Larry is passed out. Rusty is not looking forward to bringing him home.

They arrive at Larry's house, which like Rusty's, is a colonial. The boys try to rouse Larry, to no avail. So they drag his body out of the van, like a mafia hit squad, Rusty thinks, and the four carry Larry to the front door. "This is going to be awkward," mutters Rusty as he rings the doorbell.

Rusty looks up and sees a light go on in an upstairs bedroom. Seconds later, he hears footsteps descending a stairway and then the sound of locks disengaging. A striking blonde woman stands before them in a bathrobe. She gasps at the sight of Larry.

"Hi Mrs. Furillo," says Barry in a sheepish tone. "We're bringing Larry home."

"What happened to him?" his mother asks.

"I'm afraid he had a rough night," says Rusty. "Is there a sofa we can place him on?"

"Uh, yeah, sure," she responds. "Follow me."

After struggling to squeeze him and themselves through the front doorway, they follow Mrs. Furillo to a living room, where they place Larry on a sofa.

"What were you guys doing?"

After a moment of awkward silence, Barry says "We had a little bit to drink before the concert. Larry had a little bit more."

Mrs. Furillo grunts at that. "I'll say." Turning to Rusty she says pointedly "I'm surprised to see you tonight!"

Rusty shrugs with embarrassment. "Yeah, me too."

Later on, Rusty arrives at his house, having been driven home by Paul. He can see that the family room light is on, which means his mom is up waiting for him. Rusty is not surprised. He had to do some convincing to get permission to attend this concert.

Rusty enters the house and goes straight upstairs to the family room where his mother sits clad in a green bathrobe. "You're a bit late!" she snaps. Well, to be fair, it is 1:30AM, Rusty thinks.

"Yes, I'm sorry Mom. I was the last guy to be dropped off." This is actually true, and she seems to accept this.

"Did you have a good time?" she asks.

"Yeah, it was a great concert."

"How's Larry?"

"Uh, he's all right."

"Really?" she asks, her eyebrows raised.

"Yeah, listen, I'm exhausted. I'd like to go straight to bed." This is also true.

"Good idea. Good night."

* * * * *

Two days later, Rusty is running in the empty hallways of Northfield High with the team captain Michael Wiseman right behind him, doing the final 660-yard or 2 hallway lap repeat of the day. At least he does not have to worry about head on collisions with other students when rounding the sharp corners. It's winter break, and while many of Rusty's teammates are away on ski holidays, Rusty and a handful of teammates are coming to late morning workouts. Larry has not shown up. Apparently, he's with his father again. Rusty wonders how he's doing after that rock concert fiasco.

Rusty and Michael come to the final straightaway, and with a final sprint, Rusty is able to hold off Wiseman. Coach Scarpella is there with his stopwatch calling off the times, Rusty finishes in 1:52. "Good job, Rusty!" says Scarpella.

Satisfied, Rusty heads into the locker room and changes. He puts his running shoes and clothes into a plastic shopping bag. Because it's the middle of the day and both his parents are working, Rusty rode his bike to get to school. He closes his locker, locks it, and heads outside. It's cold and crisp out. Rusty mounts his bike, a Schwinn ten- speeder, and sets off onto School Road, the plastic shopping bag hanging from the handlebars. He makes a right turn onto the curiously named Lord's Highway. It's not a highway at all, just another heavily wooded residential road lined with old stone walls. Rusty thinks of Carla as he rides, wondering if she's at work on her novel or a new song. He crests a hill before beginning a sharp descent.

Rusty regains consciousness lying on the pavement. His head throbs, his face and chin feel as if they're on fire, and he feels excruciating pain in his right forearm and wrist. Obviously, he has wiped out on his bike, but he has no memory of the accident.

He hears the sound of an oncoming car, and it crests the hill, clearly going faster than the 25 mile per hour speed limit. Rusty closes his eyes, bracing himself for his violent demise as he hears the brief cry of screeching tires. The car stops short by ten feet and a woman of about forty gets out.

"Oh my!" she exclaims as she hurries toward him. "Have you been here long or did this just happen?"

"I dunno," he gasps.

"I see what happened here," she says while gesturing to his bike which lies by his feet. "Your bag got caught in the spokes of the front wheel." She turns to look at Rusty. "We gotta get you to a hospital. My house is just a few houses down. I'll go call an ambulance."

She gets up and leaves. Rusty feels alone and abandoned, even though he knows that she is helping him. He begins to shake and shiver, wondering if its due to the cold or if he's going into shock.

* * * * *

Rusty lies on a gurney, his mom at his side. He's been languishing here in the Norwalk Hospital emergency room for about four hours. The only break in this monotony was being wheeled into another room to have his right forearm x-rayed. His forearm and wrist are badly swollen. This is familiar territory, unfortunately. When Rusty was in fifth grade, while he was waiting for his bus to take him home, a kid at his middle school suddenly pushed him off a ledge onto a courtyard, resulting in a fracture of his right wrist.

A man of about fifty now approaches Rusty. "Peter Rassmussen? I'm Dr. Murphy, I'm an orthopedist here and I've reviewed your x-rays. You have a displaced fracture of your right forearm. Before we can get a cast on your arm, I need to realign the bone, okay?"

Rusty silently nods his head. The doctor has the orderlies wheel Rusty into a small room not far off. Once there, Dr. Murphy gently touches Rusty's forearm, palpating it while feeling for the fracture site. Even gentle touching makes Rusty yelp and flinch. "It's okay, Peter, I'll be done soon," he says, trying to reassure him. His hands settle on his forearm before he suddenly wrenches it.

Rusty lets out a scream so intense it seems to come from the depths of his soul. Writhing in the gurney, he experiences a level of agony he never imagined possible. Rusty wonders why they can't put people under for this procedure.

"There, we're finished here," the doctor announces cheerfully. "I'll have the orderlies wheel you back to your mom." Rusty continues to writhe.

* * * * *

The next day, Rusty lies in his hospital room with both his mom and dad by his side. He's being kept here at the hospital primarily for observation due to his concussion. As time drags on, Rusty begins to realize how dull life as a hospital patient can be. Other than his parents, his only entertainment is a small black and white television set that hangs from an appendage attached to the ceiling. It enables Rusty to maneuver the screen to the best viewing angle and to manually change the channel, albeit with his left hand, which is difficult but doable. The entertainment offerings are slim: mostly game shows, soap operas, and children's shows like cartoons and *Sesame Street*. His most exciting moments of the day are when he's served meals, when a doctor or nurse examines him, and when he has to go to the toilet.

He's watching a soap opera when he hears a knock. A nurse enters and says, "Peter? You have a visitor."

It's Carla.

Rusty feels three emotions at once: shock, elation and mortification. The mortification comes because he knows he looks like hell. His face and chin were cut during the accident, he's dressed in a hospital gown, and his hair is all messed up.

"Ms. Levy, what a surprise!" his mother exclaims.

"Oh my god, Carla, I look terrible!" says Rusty, covering his face with both his left hand and his casted right arm.

"Oh Rusty, I'm so sorry, I heard about what happened." She places what appears to be a new small backpack on the floor and reaches over to Rusty's head. "Aww…let's have a look." She parts Rusty's hair to examine his face. Her touch electrifies Rusty. He looks up and sees his father's steely blue eyes watching closely.

"That is so nice of you to visit Rusty," says his mother.

"Well, how could I not? When I heard that he'd ended up in the hospital, I got very concerned, so I decided to check up." Carla turns to Rusty and asks, "So how are you managing to occupy your time here?"

"Well, it's a pretty dull experience, being a hospital patient." Rusty gestures at the television. "As you can see, the pickings are pretty slim here."

"Well, Dr. Carla has just the antidote for that!" she announces pulling something from the backpack. She hands it to Rusty. It's a paperback novel, George Orwell's *1984*.

"Oh wow, Carla! Thanks!"

"I have something else for you, this," she says, handing him the small , brand-new backpack. "Next time, carry your belongings in this instead of a shopping bag when you ride your bike."

Carla stays for another half hour. She gets along remarkably well with his mother, chatting away, but his father is silent.

* * * * *

The following week, Rusty is back at school, having spent the rest of his winter recess convalescing. He's adjusting to life with a broken wrist. Notetaking during class is difficult because he is right-handed. He can still write, but his already poor handwriting is further compromised by his cast, which forces Rusty to grip his pen or pencil in an unnatural way. Essay exams, once a strong point, are now dreaded. The good news is that none of his injuries involve his legs. He can still run. In a couple of days, he'll be competing in the league indoor track championships.

He's back at his favorite spot on the library's radiator, trying to solve algebra problems, when he hears that familiar voice say, "Rusty?"

Carla stands before him, staring at him, wearing a snug brown turtleneck sweater. Startled, Rusty straightens up. "Yes."

"How are you feeling?"

Rusty shrugs. "Okay, I guess. Notetaking is tough, because of this," he says waving his cast. "I miss playing guitar, too. Just when things were getting good on that front."

"I know! I'm so sorry about that."

"Anyway, I want to thank you for *1984*."

"Oh," she exclaims, brightening up. "How did you like it?"

"Loved it. Finished it before I left the hospital. So, Carla, do you think we'll end up like *1984*?"

"Hmm..." She pauses. "In the Soviet Union and China, I'd say yes. That model of using mass surveillance and brute force, I can see that happening in those countries. Here in America, it'll be more like Huxley's *Brave New World*. They'll control us with drugs and all sorts of pleasurable distractions."

"That doesn't sound so bad to me."

"Speaking of pleasurable distractions, I heard about Larry at the rock concert that you went to."

Rusty's jaw drops in shock. He has never told Carla about going to that concert. "How the hell did you find out about that?"

"This is a small high school," says Carla.

Jesus, talk about *1984*. She seems to have more informants than the FBI. Rusty throws his hands up and says, "Okay, so what do you want to know?"

"Well, why don't you tell me about it from your end."

Rusty tells her about the evening, and when he finishes, Carla asks "Did Paul, your driver, have anything to drink?"

"Uh, yeah, he had some," he replies uneasily.

"Rusty!"

"Yeah, I know." Rusty sighs.

"Okay, listen. I know you and Larry go back a ways, and I know he's your friend. But I am concerned. I hear stuff about him all the time. He's not doing well, Rusty. I just don't want him dragging you down with him."

"Nobody's gonna drag me down," insists Rusty.

"I hope not. So…how was the concert?"

"Pretty good!"

"Who did you see?"

"Outlaws and Molly Hatchett. Are you familiar with them?"

"Yeah," says Carla, unenthusiastic. "Southern rock isn't my cup of tea."

"What is?" asks Rusty, leaning forward, keenly interested.

"Well, as you know, I love Joni Mitchell. I like Reggae music, bands like Bob Marley and the Wailers, and Toots and the Maytals. I also like some new wave acts like Elvis Costello. I'm into some of the more recent material that Bob Dylan has put out. There are some bands in the city that I follow like the Talking Heads, New York Dolls, Patti Smith, Blondie."

"Yeah," says Rusty, nodding his head, though he knows nothing about these acts except for Blondie and Dylan.

"I have to go," says Carla. "Don't go to any more rock concerts with Larry."

"I want to go to more concerts!" says Rusty as she begins to walk away.

"Except I want to go with you!"

Carla turns her face toward Rusty, and he is rewarded with a blush and a smile.

* * * * *

Two days later, Rusty and Larry are inside the Wilton High School Field House for the Western Connecticut Conference indoor track championships. The field house is a large and impressive structure, big enough to accommodate a 160-yard track. The minty smell of Ben Gay, a ubiquitous presence at indoor track meets, fills the space as runners and jumpers apply the cream on their hamstrings to prevent muscle pulls. Rusty has watched the meet unfold while waiting for his event. The kids competing in field events have already started shot putting, pole vaulting, high jumping and long jumping. On the track, Northfield's boys' track team has already gotten off to a great start, the sprint relay team setting a meet record, and their best sprinter, a senior named Jim McMahon, won the 50-yard dash. Now, coaches and athletes are setting up hurdles for the 60-yard hurdles race. Michael Wiseman strides by and asks Larry "Ready to warm up?" Larry shrugs.

Rusty nudges Larry. "Go on, go get 'em."

With apparent reluctance, Larry gets up and joins Michael for a warm-up jog. Rusty watches them, thinking about the contrast between the two. Wiseman is likely to get into Harvard, Larry is likely to flunk out of high school. He glances at Carla, who is here with Scarpella, helping to officiate. Yesterday, her girls took the league title. He thinks about what she said about Larry. He hopes Carla is wrong, but he knows that Carla is very smart and is probably an accurate judge of people.

Once the hurdles race is completed, the kids running the mile gather at the starting line. There are about a dozen runners from various high schools. Larry and Michael are the two representing Northfield. An official gives the runners some final instructions. He then raises his starting pistol, the runners crouch. The gun is fired with a loud echoey boom, and the runners are off.

As usual, Larry shoots out to the lead from the start. He has always done that, to Coach Scarpella's frustration. He has no sense of pacing whatsoever. Larry usually does okay until the last lap or two. This time, he's breathing heavily after two laps, which is a problem, since this is a ten-lap race. A runner for Bethel passes him at lap four, and Wiseman passes him at lap five. After that, one by one the other runners overtake him. By the eighth lap, Larry is in last place. Wiseman finishes second, Larry jogs to the finish.

Rusty thinks of maybe going over to Larry and saying something to him, but he is intercepted by Coach Scarpella. "How ya doin'?" he asks Rusty, slapping him on the shoulder.

"Okay, coach."

"Good. Go get yourself warmed up. You got a tough race ahead of you."

Rusty sheds his sweatpants and sweat jacket, though getting the sleeve over his cast is accomplished with difficulty. He begins to jog along the inside of the track and within a minute into his jog he encounters his rival and nemesis, Trevor Levelle.

Trevor is of medium height, and of a heavier build then Rusty. He sports a shaggy mane of blond hair and he would not look out of place on a rock band's album cover. The two know each other now that they have raced in various track meets over the past year. Trevor stares at Rusty. "What happened to you?"

"Bike accident."

"And you're still running?"

"I'm only a mess from the waist up. My legs are just fine."

"Man, you're hardcore, dude," says Trevor, shaking his head and smiling.

Me? A hardcore dude? Rusty smiles back.

The two jog together for a while before all the runners are called in. Rusty learns that there will be two heats. Rusty and Trevor are in the first, or fast heat. Trevor is assigned lane three, Rusty, lane four. The official orders the runners to line up according to their assignments. He then says "Runners, on your marks." Rusty and his competitors crouch down. "Stead-eee!"

The gun goes off.

Rusty quickly settles in the pack while Trevor surges ahead. It feels strange racing with his arm in a cast. Halfway around the track, he sees Carla, who is holding a stopwatch. "Come on Rusty, you got this!" she shouts. Feeling energized, he waits for the short straightaway before surging past a runner and then settles behind another. He repeats the process, again and again, before he finds himself in second place, behind Trevor, who is far ahead. Rusty notes his strange style of running in an erect stance. He wonders how is he able to go so fast running like that. Rusty has less than two laps to go, there is no way he'll catch him, but he surges anyway, to try to get closer, and to maintain his second-place position. His lungs burn as he sprints the final lap. As he rounds the final turn, he sees Trevor cross the finish line. About eight seconds later, Rusty finishes as well. Carla trots over to him.

"Rusty, I got you in 2:28.2."

"Yes!" exclaims Rusty, for this is a personal best for him at this distance. The two raise their hands in triumph and then they spontaneously hug. It's a brief and platonic embrace, but Rusty feels the contours of her body press against him, and he is instantly aroused. He's wearing running shorts, and an erection will be spotted a mile away. Rusty smiles at Carla, says "Thank you," then sprints over to where he left his sweats. He hurriedly puts them on before he receives congratulations from his teammates.

MARCH 1979

On a cold Saturday evening, Rusty and his parents are standing outside the Fine Arts Cinema in Westport. They are about to see *The Deer Hunter*, a film set during the Vietnam War. Rusty has been eager to see this film since it was released last December.

Once they are in the theatre and have claimed their seats, Rusty runs back to the concession area to buy his soda and popcorn and then rejoins his parents. The film starts slowly, showing a group of friends who are steel workers in Pennsylvania, led by a character named Michael, who is played by Robert De Niro. There is a long scene in which one of the characters gets married.

Then the film cuts to Vietnam, where three of the characters, including Michael, are serving. The three are captured and forced by their captors to play Russian Roulette. The Russian roulette scene is one of the scariest and most riveting scenes Rusty has ever experienced, and it's also the most gratifying—when De Niro and a friend turn the guns on their tormentors.

The scene that affects Rusty most, though, is when Michael returns home from Vietnam. He blows off a welcome home party and instead checks into a motel. As these scenes unfold, a beautiful classical guitar piece plays in the background. Rusty is moved by the music. Until now, Rusty's musical interests have been rock and recently bluegrass, because of playing with Kevin. Now he finds himself wanting to learn how to play this style of music. He can't wait to get this damned cast off.

The film is three hours long. At the end, Rusty is both wired and exhausted; wired because of the intense Russian roulette scenes, exhausted by the sheer length of the film. He has to pee, though he stays to watch the final credits. He finds out the name of the song he liked was "Cavatina."

After emerging from the bathroom, Rusty finds his dad standing alone, waiting for Mom. He joins him and looks around before noticing a young couple approaching them on their way out. The woman is Carla. She sees Rusty and walks right over. "Rusty, what a surprise!"

"Yeah," says Rusty, who is both stunned and disheartened to see Carla with another man. "Hell of a movie, huh?"

"I thought it was awful!"

"Really? Why?"

"The film was way too long. The wedding scene by itself could have been cut in half. And, it's historically inaccurate. Neither the North Vietnamese nor the Viet Cong ever forced their prisoners to play Russian roulette!"

Rusty gives a quick glance at her companion, a handsome enough guy who stands tight lipped behind her. "Oh, this is my friend Brian," she says. Brian reaches over to shake Rusty's hand. Rusty offers his casted hand.

"Bike accident," he explains.

"So, how did you like it?" Carla asks Rusty.

"Oh, I don't know. I was struck by the friendship of these men, particularly Michael's devotion to Nick. I mean, he traveled halfway around the world and played Russian roulette with him to try to save him. That's devotion. I found that pretty powerful."

"Hmm...that's an interesting point."

Rusty's mom has arrived. "Well, hello, Ms. Levy!" she says.

"Hi Mrs. Rassmussen," replies Carla, who then turns to Rusty. "We should talk more about this later. I'll see you at school?"

"Yeah, sure." He watches Carla and her date walk out the door and thinks: *I'm completely broken. I have a broken wrist, and now I've got a broken heart.* Yet he feels a glimmer of hope. She said she wants to talk about the film some more.

Rusty sits in the back seat of their Ford Pinto as they drive home. Well, of course. Carla is a beautiful, talented woman in her early twenties, and she is a faculty member of his high school. To say that she's out of his league would be a gross understatement.

His father breaks the silence by saying, "I see that Ms. Levy has a boyfriend."

Gee Dad, thanks for rubbing it in.

* * * * *

Rusty sits in the living room watching an episode of *The White Shadow*, a TV series about a white basketball coach teaching kids in the inner city, though not all of the players are Black. One of them, a player named Goldstein, is Jewish, and there is an Italian kid named "Salami." Rusty wonders how realistic this show is, but he enjoys it nonetheless. The phone rings, its sound strident and intrusive. Mom jumps up to answer it. Usually the caller is her sister or some other relative. Even if the caller is on dad's side of the family, Mom will do most of the talking, since Dad seems averse to any phone conversation at all.

Mom returns from the kitchen. "Peter, it's for you."

Rusty trots over to the kitchen. "Hello?"

"Rusty, long time no talk to." It's Travis, his guitar teacher.

"Hey Travis, what's up?"

"I was wondering when I'll be seeing you again. How's your wrist?"

"I've got a few more weeks, till early April, when I see the doctor and he'll cut off the cast."

"You okay?" Travis asks.

Damn, that guy doesn't miss a thing, even on the phone. Rusty lets out a sigh. "Well, yeah. It's kind of stupid."

"Talk to me Rusty. What's goin' on?"

"Well, remember that hot-looking teacher I've been telling you about?"

"The Divine Carla Levy?"

"Yeah, her. I ran into her at the movies the other night. She had a date."

"Aha," says Travis.

"I don't know...I mean, she's so gorgeous, of course she's going to meet and date men, and what am I? A sixteen-year-old nobody."

"You are not a nobody," retorts Travis. "Get that out of your head. You are sixteen years old though. That's a fact."

"Yeah, I guess you're right about that."

"So, what were they like together?"

Rusty frowns. "What do you mean?"

"Were they lovey-dovey with each other? Were they kissing, holding hands, anything like that?"

"Well, no, not at all. She was yammering on about how much she hated the movie, and he was just standing there, not saying anything."

"Hmm." After a pause Travis says, "I think you're still in the running, buddy."

"Really?"

"Yeah. She ain't into him."

* * * * *

Rusty and Larry are once again in Larry's Chevy Blazer hurtling through the streets of Northfield. They are on their way to a party at some senior's house. House parties are a social high point here in Northfield, due to its lack of other diversions for teens. They generally happen when a kid's parents decide to decamp for a weekend, unwisely leaving the teenager behind. He or she will then pool resources with friends and arrange to buy several kegs of beer, legally if the one purchasing the booze is 18. Through the word-of-mouth rumor mill of high school communication, the student body knows of the festivities. An admission of $2 is charged. If enough kids show up, the hosts stand to make a profit.

Rusty has been to only one of these parties before, last year, at the end of his freshman year. Usually, they seem to happen the night before a big cross-country or track meet, so he passes. He's allowing himself this diversion since now he's in between indoor and outdoor track seasons. Rusty also wants to distract himself from his continuing distress at seeing Carla at the movies with a date.

"You know where this place is?" asks Rusty.

"Yeah, on Steep Hill Road," replies Larry. Rusty knows the road from cross-country team training runs. It's aptly named.

Larry turns onto Steep Hill Road, and after driving a few hundred yards, they see cars parked on the side of the road. Larry pulls over and parks behind the nearest vehicle.

They get out of the car and walk toward the sound of Lynyrd Skynyrd being blasted from stereo speakers a couple hundred feet away. They find the house, yet another colonial. There are a few kids standing outside conversing, drinking and smoking weed, but most of the action is inside. They proceed to the door, where a high school senior Rusty vaguely knows is standing at the threshold, taking money. Rusty and Larry each pay $2, and they walk in.

Inside, the house is packed with kids. Rusty makes his way through the house until he finds the kegs. While familiar with the concept of kegs, he has never served himself beer from one before. He grabs a plastic cup, takes the faucet that is attached to the keg via a tube, presses the lever and begins to pour, and a white foam collects in the cup. An older kid says to Rusty "No, not like that. You got to tilt it like this," showing him the proper angle. "Otherwise, you get nothing but foam."

Rusty does as instructed and is rewarded with a full cup of beer.

"Thanks," he says.

Rusty turns and sees that Larry's gone. He thinks about looking for him but decides that maybe he should try to mingle with other kids, maybe even talk to a girl. But instead, he stands alone awkwardly for a long time. In high school, trying to interact with anyone outside your clique just feels impossible. He learned that lesson at the dance a couple of months ago, and he's learning it here, even with the social lubricant of beer. He walks around the confines of the house a couple of times before he decides to look for Larry.

Rusty ascends a stairway to see if Larry's on the second floor. There are several bedrooms in this rather large house, and at one of them he hears muffled voices. Rusty opens the door and see several kids, mostly boys, including Larry. He sits on the floor, his back propped up against a bed, and he looks up at Rusty with glassy eyes like he had at the rock concert. Smiling, Larry says, "What's up?"

"Not much. You alright?"

"I just did some Quaaludes."

"Oh Jesus," Rusty mutters. This is a problem. No way I'm going home with him like that, he thinks.

"Listen, Larry, I'm going to bail. I'll head back home somehow. You take care."

"Right," says Larry.

Rusty leaves the room but pauses outside in the hallway. How the hell am I going to get home? He could look for a phone and call his mom for a ride home, but that would mean explaining why Larry is not driving him home in the first place. The party is still in full swing, so he doubts he can bum a ride off anyone else. The only other option is by foot. He is easily a couple of miles from home, maybe farther, but if he jogs at least part of the way, he can make it home by around midnight maybe, and not get in trouble with his mom.

A few hundred yards into his homeward journey, Rusty wonders if he's made a mistake. The road is unlit, windy and lacks shoulders, so Rusty has to jump in the bushes each time a car approaches to avoid getting killed. He's also not completely sure if he knows how to get home. Rusty looks ahead and again sees the power lines lit up, the harbinger of a vehicle coming around the corner.

Rusty jumps in the bushes again. Three cars pass by, all of them police cars. *Uh-oh*, Rusty thinks. The party's being busted. Some neighbor must have complained about the noise. He wonders how Larry's going to fare now that he's messed up on Quaaludes and possibly booze as well. Not his problem now.

Rusty comes to the end of a road, and he sees the Saugatuck Reservoir out in the moonlit distance. Now he knows his way back home. He soon comes to Godfrey Road, which will lead him back to his street. He still has over a mile to go, but now he feels energized and he jogs most of the way home.

He arrives at his house a few minutes past midnight. His mom is once again in the family room waiting for him, watching *Saturday Night Live*. Rusty smiles at this. Once, *Saturday Night Live* had been a secret guilty pleasure of his. He would set his alarm for 11:25pm and tip toe down the stairs while his parents slept, and he would watch the show with the volume turned way down. One evening during his freshman year, his mom came down the stairs. For a moment, Rusty thought he was going to get scolded. Instead, she was intrigued, and she sat down and watched it with him.

"How was the party, Rusty?" she asks.

"It was okay," he replies. He glances at the TV. Gilda Radner is on, doing her Roseanne Rosannadanna routine, going off on a lengthy tangent about bodily functions. Rusty grins at his mom. "Mind if I join you?"

* * * * *

It's the end of the month on a brisk Friday afternoon. Rusty is headed to the high school gym locker room. Outdoor track season is just starting. Rusty and his teammates will be working out on the roads for now, as the cinder surface of the track is too soft and muddy for running.

Rusty walks down the hallway. Just before reaching the entrance, he sees Carla. Looking at him, she says, "Hi Rusty." She looks unhappy and troubled in some way. Oh Christ, I hope she didn't find out about that stupid party, even though nothing bad had happened to Larry.

"How's it going? You okay?" he asks.

"Yeah, I'm fine. I'm just upset about the news lately."

Rusty is puzzled. "Hmm...the news. Oh, you mean that accident? Um, Three Mile Island, right?"

"Yes, Rusty, Three Mile Island. I have always been against nuclear power.

I was involved with the anti-nuclear movement when I was in college."

"Really?" asks Rusty, curious.

"Well, I come from a family of political activists. I feel I should do my part somehow."

"Too bad you weren't here last year."

"Why's that?" she asks.

"We had some guy speak here. He was a student at Princeton who designed an atomic bomb."

"Oh yeah, John Aristotle Phillips, 'The A-Bomb Kid.' I know of him. What did you think?"

"Well, it was a scary story. After he designed it, the Pakistanis wanted to buy his design."

"It *is* a scary story Rusty, like this accident."

"I guess I'll have to see *The China Syndrome*," Rusty says, referring to the film about an accident at a nuclear power plant, which had opened only a couple of weeks earlier.

"Yes, talk about a well-timed film release," says Carla, her expression brightening. "Hey, I'll see you at practice?" she asks, reaching out and touching his arm.

"Yeah, sure."

Rusty watches Carla as she walks off. His mind races. *Oh my god, is Travis right? Am I still in the running?*

APRIL 1979

During his free period, Rusty sits in his favorite spot, on top of the radiator in the library, writing in his notebook, albeit clumsily. He's never quite gotten the hang of writing with his casted wrist. In a few days the cast will be coming off. He'll miss looking at the signatures on it, especially Carla's.

"Well, hello."

Rusty turns and it's Carla, smiling. Rusty is pleasantly surprised and happy that he is interacting with her again.

"I see you're at your usual spot, but wait! No unassigned book? You're actually working on something?"

Rusty laughs. "Yeah, working on this damned sophomore paper."

"What's your paper going to be about?"

"Upton Sinclair's *The Jungle*. God, what a depressing novel."

"A good choice though," replies Carla. "It's a socially important novel, and it led to changes. You've read the novel, right?"

"Yeah," replies Rusty. "I got a handle on the novel. I'm worried about the paper. It's got to be ten pages! I've never done anything like that before, and I'm a lousy writer."

"Hmm...I have an idea. You're writing it now, right?"

"Yes."

"Okay then. Finish writing the paper, type it up, and I'll take a look at it."

Rusty is astounded. "You serious? You'll do that for me?"

"Of course! But remember, you'll have to revise it, which means you'll have to rewrite it and type it again."

"Oh," replies Rusty, the enormity of this task beginning to weigh on him. Carla's offer of salvation has a caveat: he'll have to devote far more time to this assignment than he anticipated. Deflated, he says, "Okay, I'll get it to you."

He finishes the long-hand part of the task two days later. The next few evenings test Rusty's patience and resolve. Fortunately, he is able to use his mother's electric typewriter. It's an incredible machine, vastly preferable to the clunky manual one. Still, Rusty keeps making typing errors almost every other word, and typing with his casted arm only adds to the awkwardness. His mom had trained at a secretarial school last year and was able to type 40 words per minute, which seems inconceivable to Rusty. He thought of asking his mom to type it, but given that she works all day and then cooks dinner afterward, he decided against it. He resolves to take a typing class next year.

And so it goes, night after night, Rusty typing in a hunt-and-peck style, pausing every couple of words to erase his latest mistake. Finally, after three evenings of hard labor, he finds Carla in the faculty lounge, where she accepts his first draft with a smile.

The next day, Rusty is at his locker between classes when he hears the now familiar voice say "Rusty?"

Rusty turns and sees Carla brandishing his term paper. "I went over your paper. You are not a lousy writer, but this needs a lot of work." She hands it over to him. Rusty looks it over and to his dismay, sees that all the pages are covered in red ink. Oh god, it's a total rewrite. *I don't have time for this shit!* He looks up at Carla and is about to protest, but her stern expression precludes this. "Just follow my directions, Rusty. If you do, you'll get an excellent grade, I promise."

Deflated again, Rusty manages to say, "Okay, Carla, thank you."

* * * * *

Rusty heads back to the locker room with his teammates after finishing his workout, which was eight sets of 440s. He felt pretty strong during the workout, but now his legs are shot. As usual, Rusty has finished the workout too late for the late bus. He used to be able to count on Larry to give him a ride home, but now that Larry's been skipping workouts, Rusty no longer has that option. So, after changing his clothes, he has to head to the coach's office to phone his mom and ask for a pickup. At least his cast is off. He's looking forward to coming home and playing his guitar before walking the dog and doing homework.

Rusty walks inside and sees Carla there. She smiles at Rusty. "What brings you here?" she asks.

"I gotta call my mom. She's my ride home."

"Didn't you say she's got a job somewhere?"

"Yeah, she works until 5:00. She doesn't get here till 5:15."

"That's craziness! I'll drive you home."

"What? Really?" stammers Rusty.

"Sure. Let's go."

Stunned, he follows her outside to the faculty parking area. Wow, first she helps me with my sophomore paper, and now this? There's her car, a blue Volkswagon Beetle. He has to move the passenger seat back all the way before he can fit his long frame inside.

Carla reaches down after turning on the ignition and activates her tape deck. A song that Rusty is not familiar with begins. In the opening lines, the singer laments that attractive women are walking down the street with men who apparently look like gorillas. Rusty breaks out in laughter.

"Like that, huh?" says Carla.

"Yup," admits Rusty. He eventually hears the chorus to "Is She Really Going Out with Him?"

"Is that a song you can relate to?" asks Carla.

"Yeah, you can say that," he replies, thinking of the guy he saw Carla with, who was not a gorilla, but whatever. "Who's this?"

"Joe Jackson," replies Carla. "I love his songwriting. Get his album!"

"Okay, I will." Rusty is so enamored of Carla that he will take any recommendations from her.

He directs Carla to his house. When Carla stops the car at the end of the driveway, he turns and sees her smiling. She appears impressed by what she sees. "Is this your place?"

"Yes, it is. You want to have a look?"

"Definitely!"

Rusty gets out of the car and leads her to the backyard. The property behind his house is bisected by a brook. The back yard just outside the house is a grass lawn, while the area beyond the brook is woodland. Ferns and skunk cabbage are shooting up alongside the creek and the leaves on the trees are just beginning to emerge.

"It's beautiful, Rusty!" Carla exclaims. "I can only imagine how verdant your property will become in a few weeks."

"Verdant?" Rusty asks, unsure of the word.

"Meaning covered with green vegetation."

"You want to sit, hang out for a bit?"

"OK." They head over to a spot near the stream and sit on the grass. Carla still appears impressed.

"What?" asks Rusty.

"You don't understand, Rusty, I'm a city girl. I've lived in apartments all my life. I've never lived in a house with property like this." This comment startles Rusty and causes him to realize that up to now he has never really thought about his living situation. This house and its surrounding property happen to be where he grew up. Carla's reaction to seeing his place makes him realize just how fortunate and privileged he is.

"How long have you lived here?" Carla asks.

"We moved here just before I turned seven. We're originally from Illinois, near Chicago. My dad got transferred here."

"Do you remember Illinois?"

"Yeah, a little bit. It was a nice place, too, but different. We had a ranch style house, everything on one floor, except for the basement. We didn't have wooded land like this. It was more open, prairie like."

"Do you miss it there?"

"Nah," Rusty replies. "I was really young when we moved here. This house here is the only home I've ever really known. I think my mom misses Illinois, though. Most of her family still lives out there. A lot of her old friends, too."

A brief silence ensues. There's a question that Rusty has been meaning to ask for a while.

"So, how's it going with that guy I met?"

"What guy?"

"You know, the guy who was with you at the movies last month? I thought he might be your boyfriend."

"Oh, that guy," Carla replies. "No, he's not my boyfriend. He's just a guy I went out with."

"Oh," replies Rusty, feeling relieved, and probably doing a poor job of disguising his relief. Carla smiles at Rusty.

"What about you? Do you have a girlfriend?"

"Oh, God no."

"I bet there're plenty of girls that would love to go out with you."

Rusty can feel himself blush. "Nah, nobody I know of." But then he remembers. "Well, unless you count the girl who lives back there," he says, jerking his thumb in the direction of a neighbor's house.

"And who would that be, pray tell?"

"Oh, that's Tracy Thomas. She's a neighbor of ours."

"Does she have a crush on you?"

"Yeah, kids tease me about it all the time. She has a sidekick, another neighbor named Paula. They do things like call me up on the phone and hang up. I know it's them because I hear nervous giggling before the line goes dead. Sometimes they follow me while I'm walking the dog."

"And you're not interested in her?"

"No, not really."

"Why? Do you find her unattractive? Is she not your type?"

Rusty grimaces as he struggles to articulate a good answer. "She's okay. It's just...well, she's only a year younger than me, but she looks way younger than that, like she's in sixth grade or something. If I dated her, it'd be like molesting a child." He lets out a sigh and throws his hand forward in that universal sign of despair. "Ugh. She'll probably be a total babe when she grows up."

Carla bursts out in laughter so loud it startles Rusty, since he didn't think he had said anything that was that funny. "She just might, you know!" she exclaims. After a momentary pause she says "Actually, I was a lot like that girl when I was her age. I was really into boys, and I didn't develop breasts until I was 16."

Rusty is surprised at this revelation. "Wow, I suppose your life got a lot more interesting after that."

"Yeah, well, it kind of put the kibosh on my budding track career."

"You ran track as a girl?"

"Yes, Rusty. I was a sprinter. 100 and 220."

"Were you a fast girl?" Rusty asks. Carla laughs at that, and Rusty realizes his slip. "I'm sorry, I meant..."

"It's okay, Rusty. Yes, I was the fastest sprinter on the track team. I even ran the anchor leg on the relay team."

"Wow," says Rusty. Suddenly, he straightens up and turns to Carla. "You know what? I just realized something. He we are, sitting here face to face in my backyard, I've known you since the beginning of the school year, and I still don't know much of anything about you."

"What would you like to know about me?" she asks, her eyes wide open.

"Hmm, okay. How do you like working here as a teacher?"

Carla leans back, considering her answer. "It's nice, I like it. Though it's the whitest place I've ever been to."

"What do you mean?"

"It's homogenous. There's scarcely anyone here from different racial backgrounds."

"We have some Jewish kids here."

Carla's eyes open wide in mock surprise. "Ooooo, ooooo, such diversity! I'm Jewish, too, you know!"

Rusty laughs.

"Tell me," She continues, "How many Black kids are here?"

"Um, I think two, and they're from the same family."

"Uh-huh. And how many Puerto Ricans or other Spanish-speaking people?"

"Um, only one."

"Anybody here of Asian descent? Chinese? Japanese?"

"Nope," Rusty admits.

"Right. That's been my big culture shock coming here."

"Ah, I see. All right. Here's another question. Tell me about your parents."

"My dad is a labor lawyer. He represents labor unions. He also happens to be a high-ranking member of the Communist Party."

"What? Your dad is a commie?" gasps Rusty, unable to control his reaction.

"Yup, he is. That makes me a red diaper baby. Does that bother you?"

Rusty bursts out laughing. He finds the phrase hilarious. "You're a what?"

"A red diaper baby. That is a daughter or a son of a communist. Does that bother you?" she asks again.

"Oh no, just surprised, I guess. I've never met anyone who was one." After a moment he asks, "Are you a communist?"

"Me? No." She appears to be on the verge of laughter, as if she enjoys shocking Rusty.

"What about your mom? Is she a communist?"

"Nope. She's an English professor at Sarah Lawrence, a small liberal arts college. I'd say she's too much of a bohemian free spirit to be any kind of radical. She's originally from England."

"Really?"

"Yes. I am actually descended from Jews who immigrated from the Middle East. My mother's side came from Egypt and settled in England. My dad's family came to America from what is now Syria. My mom and one of her sisters were sent over here to live with relatives in New York during the Blitz, and that's how she met my dad. Anyway, she's been here ever since. She still speaks with an English accent." Carla utters her last sentence in an apparent imitation of her mother.

"Do you have any brothers or sisters?" Rusty asks.

"I have two younger sisters, no brothers. One is in art school. The other is in the High School of Performing Arts in the city. She wants to make it on Broadway."

"I have one sister, older," says Rusty. "She's also is trying to make it as an actress." After a brief pause, he asks, "So what made you decide to become a teacher?"

"I guess the profession appeals to my idealistic nature. I want to impart my love of literature and language to my students. Plus, those school breaks are great for focusing on my writing."

"I can't wait to read your first novel."

"Well, don't hold your breath." After a beat, she asks "So, what do you want to be after college?"

Rusty considers this. "Oh, I don't know. I think I'd like to do something in the medical field. I can't see myself getting into medical school, but maybe some other job where I'm helping people somehow."

"You should be a social worker—I can see you doing that. A cousin of mine whom I'm close to is one. He's a handsome, kind, athletic guy like you."

This spate of complimentary adjectives coming from Carla causes Rusty to blush, especially the first one. He is not at all sure about how to respond, but he manages to say "Well, coming from such a beautiful girl, I mean woman, like you..."

Carla immediately leans toward Rusty. "Do you really think I'm beautiful?"

"Yes, yes, of course. Why wouldn't I? I mean, isn't it obvious?"

"That's so sweet. Thank you." She runs her fingers through Rusty's thick thatch of red hair. She is leaning closer now, looking directly at him. *Oh my God, are we going to kiss?*

And then they do.

Rusty feels Carla's lips on his, and they feel wet and rubbery. He also feels the flow of warm air coming from her nose on his face. He feels both disoriented and profoundly aroused. After a few seconds she gently pulls away, and she appears stunned, though he doubts that she's anywhere as shocked as he. She again moves in, and they kiss again. This time, it's a more forceful and longer lasting kiss. When she pulls away again, she asks, "You're not going to tell anyone about this, are you?"

"Oh, no."

"Don't tell Larry."

"Oh, God no!" he gasps.

She smiles at this. "I've got to go. Your mom is going to be home soon, right?"

"Yeah."

Rusty walks Carla to her car. He watches as she gets into her VW, starts it, and maneuvers it in the driveway. She looks at Rusty one last time and flashes a smile.

* * * * *

Rusty once again sits atop the radiator in the library. He is sleep-deprived, keyed up after kissing Carla. He feels wired. He desperately wants to see her again and hopes to God that she will offer him a ride home. Maybe he can show Carla the inside of the house, take her upstairs to his bedroom...

"Hi, Rusty."

It was only a whisper, but Carla's greeting startles Rusty so completely that he loses his grip on his algebra textbook, and it falls to the floor with a thud. Carla covers her mouth and begins laughing, and then so does Rusty.

"I'm sorry, Rusty. I didn't mean to scare you."

"It's okay," he says smiling, before reaching down to retrieve his textbook. "How are you doing?"

"Listen, I've got a ton of papers and tests to grade, and I won't be able to give you a ride."

"Oh, okay," replies Rusty, trying to conceal his disappointment.

"But tomorrow is Saturday. I was wondering if you would like to meet me someplace."

"I'd love that. There's not much to do here though. What do you like to do?"

Carla smiles. "Well, I love hiking. A city girl like me loves fresh air."

Rusty considers this. "Hmm...Hey, I got an idea!"

"What?"

"There's this big nature preserve not too far my house called Devil's

Den. It's not too far from here, maybe a couple of miles. Plenty of trails."

"How would I get there?"

"Hmm…Let me draw you a map." Rusty reaches for his notebook and tears out a sheet of paper. Rusty's drawing skills are rudimentary, but fortunately, getting there is a simple process.

"What time do you want to meet?" he asks.

"Is two o'clock okay?"

"Yeah, sure."

"Are you sure it's okay?" Carla asks.

"Yeah, it's only a mile and a half from my house, really easy by bike. I'll tell my folks that I'm going out for a bike ride. I do that a lot on weekends, so it's not unusual."

"Okay then, see you tomorrow?"

"Yeah, tomorrow at two."

"Good." Carla smiles and turns away.

Yes!

* * * * *

Saturday afternoon finds Rusty on his bike riding on Godfrey Road toward the Devil's Den nature preserve. He knows the preserve well; his parents have taken him there on weekend hikes throughout his childhood and adolescence. This is the first time he is going there with anyone else.

Rusty makes a right turn on Pent Road and takes it to the end where the preserve's parking lot is located. He parks his bike, locks it, and waits nervously for Carla. After about ten minutes, she arrives. Rusty can see her smiling through the windshield before she parks.

Carla gets out of her vehicle and the two gaze and smile at each other. She is wearing blue jeans and a cardigan sweater over a tight-fitting T-shirt. Rusty becomes instantly aroused at the sight. "Hi," Rusty murmurs.

"Hi, Rusty." After a beat, she says, "I've brought some snacks along. Just some trail mix and a bottle of water."

"Okay, great, thanks." After a pause, he asks, "Ready to walk?"

"Sure!"

As they begin, Rusty tells Carla the history of Devil's Den, explaining that it was the location of various mills in the late 18th and 19th centuries. Rusty first leads her to the remains of a sawmill, then takes her down a path across a stone dam of Godfrey Pond, a mill pond built in the 1700s. They stop so Carla can gaze at the pond.

"I don't suppose you can swim here, could you?" she asks with a mischievous smile.

"I think it's prohibited. You thinking of going in? It's still only April. The water is probably freezing!"

"True. Still, I love swimming in ponds and rivers like this. Especially places where you're not supposed to swim." This earns Carla a long, astonished look from Rusty. He has never seen this naughty girl side of her. He would not mind seeing her in a bikini, he muses.

They continue their hike. As they walk, Rusty learns about Carla's life. She grew up in a Brooklyn neighborhood called Park Slope. She attended Hunter High School and then Brooklyn College. After graduation, she took a teaching job in a high school in the Bronx, an experience she found traumatizing. "It wasn't just the fights you had to break up. It was this sense of hopelessness there, and that just led to a lack of motivation to learn." She lasted two years before coming to Northfield.

After hiking a couple of miles, they begin a steady climb until they reach a vista with a view of the Saugatuck Reservoir and of hills and woodland beyond. Carla gasps. Her eyes brim with tears. "Oh, Rusty, it's so beautiful! Thank you for taking me here and showing me this." She leans toward Rusty and puts her arm around his waist. Rusty in turn wraps his arm around her shoulders. It's the first time that he has seen Carla become emotional, and he's surprised and moved. Together they stand, taking in the view. After a moment, he turns to Carla, and finds her looking at him with a longing that thrills Rusty. They kiss for a moment before they hear the sound of approaching voices. A family of hikers appears, a couple with three kids, two boys and a girl. Carla blushes. "Maybe now is the time to have a snack."

After they finish eating, Rusty and Carla head back down the trail. This time it's Rusty's turn to tell her about events in his life, including family camping trips throughout the eastern U.S. and Canada, plus the various campouts when he was in the boy scouts. He mentions some of his other activities, such as his guitar lessons with Travis. At no point does he bring up Larry. Why bring up such a depressing subject on such a beautiful day?

They eventually return to the parking lot. Carla turns to Rusty. She has a nervous expression. Rusty asks, "Something wrong?"

"Remember that guy you saw me with at the movies?"

"Yeah." *Uh-oh.*

"Turns out he was married."

Rusty is unable to conceal his shock. "Really?"

"Yeah."

"Wow! I'm sorry."

"Don't be. I wasn't in love with him. I just hate it when people are deceptive."

"Well, at least you don't have to worry about that with me."

Carla laughs. "What? You being married, or being deceptive?"

Rusty laughs and blushes. "Well, both."

"Well, you seem like an open and honest person to me. And as for you being married..." They both disintegrate into laughter. When they compose themselves, Carla says, "Thank you for the hike, Rusty. I had a wonderful time."

"Yeah, me too."

Carla reaches for both of his hands, and she pulls him closer. They kiss for a long time. "See you at school," she says.

After Rusty watches Carla drive away, he looks at his watch. *Yikes!* 5:35. He has to hurry home to walk the dog before dinner if he doesn't want to get in trouble.

* * * * *

Rusty sits in the Ford Pinto as his father drives him to his Sunday afternoon guitar lesson. His mind races. Despite repeatedly pleasuring himself last night, he was unable to sleep.

"So, how's Ms. Levy doing?" his father asks. Rusty nearly jerks up in the passenger seat.

"Um...what do you mean?"

"Oh, I don't know. I was just wondering about her. Do you know if she still has a boyfriend?"

Rusty considers his response. He decides that no harm will come with the truth. "Uh, no, apparently not. Just a one-time thing, or so she told me."

"She told you that?" asks his father. "Why is she telling you about her dating life?"

Rusty feels his insides tighten. Maybe harm does come with the truth. "I don't know, dad, maybe because I asked her."

"I see," responds his father. After a few moments of uncomfortable silence, he asks, "Where were you yesterday afternoon?"

"Um, I rode my bike to Devil's Den. Then I took a walk on the trails."

"Were you by yourself?"

"Yes," Rusty responds, inwardly wincing at his lie.

"You were gone for a very long time."

Rusty is now completely unsettled by this conversation, which is really more an interrogation. His father's tone is calm and not at all accusatory, but it is definitely probing. It reminds Rusty of some old World War II drama, when the Gestapo interrogator calmy says, "We have ways of making you talk."

Rusty is on edge for the remainder of the thankfully short trip. His father has no further questions about her or his hike.

When he enters Travis's house, his teacher looks at him and says, "You've got that 'I've Just Seen a Face' kind of look." They had worked on the Beatles song nearly a year ago.

"Really?"

Travis nods.

"Well, I guess there's a reason for that. Can you keep a secret?"

"Yeah, sure, buddy."

Rusty pauses again. "I kissed Carla."

"What?"

"We kissed. Carla and I have been making out. Nothing more than that, but yeah."

"Holy shit," mutters Travis, his hand traveling to his forehead. "When did this start?"

"A few days ago." Rusty tells Travis of his ride home with Carla and what happened later after their hike in Devil's Den.

"She's not married, right?"

"No, she's not."

"And she ain't your teacher, right?"

"Right."

"Well, okay then." Travis takes a deep breath and continues. "But man, be careful. She's still a faculty member in your school. She could get in trouble, and so could you. Have you told anyone else about this?"

"No."

"Good, keep it that way. Feel free to talk to me about it, but don't say anything to anyone else." Travis shakes his head and says, "Man, I just hope your heart doesn't get broken. In the real world, most relationships end with a breakup. You can trust me on that one."

MAY 1979

Rusty is on the track with Wiseman and a few other teammates doing sets of 440s and 220s. His mind is everywhere but on the track.

For the past week, Rusty has been on a roller coaster of emotions. First excitement and anticipation right after that first kiss and the hike in Devil's Den. But lately he has been feeling a creeping fear and disappointment, for there has been no follow through. Rusty and Carla have acknowledged each other at track practice, and he's seen her in the hallways and faculty office. He even spotted her with Mrs. Kingsley, playing tennis on the courts that are adjacent to the track. He hasn't been able to approach her because every time he sees her, she's with someone else.

Rusty is especially worried now that Carla hasn't surprised him in the library or at his locker. He wonders if Carla has changed her mind about him. He prays that it's not the case, but he wants to know one way or another. The uncertainty is killing him.

"So, what's going on with your friend Larry?" asks Wiseman as they do a recovery lap just before doing another 440.

"I don't know, Mike."

"I've been hearing all sorts of strange shit about him. I hear he's doing Quaaludes, hanging out with some sleazy people. He hasn't shown up for practice or classes in how long? He's your friend, Raz, haven't you talked to him about this?"

Wiseman's question makes Rusty feel defensive. He wants to say I'm his friend, not his fucking daddy, but decides against it. Instead, as he ponders a response, he watches Carla off in the distance, talking to a visibly exhausted female runner. "I don't know, Mike, maybe I should say something." After a pause he adds, "I think I'm losing him."

After finishing his final repeat, Rusty dejectedly jogs back to the locker room. After changing, he heads to the coach's office to call his mom. As he reaches for the phone, he hears a voice behind him say "Rusty!"

Rusty turns around and sees Carla standing at the threshold. "You okay?"

"Yeah, sure," Rusty lies.

"You need a ride?"

"Um, sure." *Oh, thank God!*

They walk to her car, and Carla tells Rusty how busy she's been as an explanation for her absence. Once they're inside her car, she again reaches down to her tape deck before pulling out of the lot. The time it's an acoustic and bluesy sounding tune, featuring a singer with a girlish, baby doll voice singing in a stream of consciousness sort of way about a friend of hers who has fallen in love.

The song sounds very familiar to Rusty, and he's certain he's heard it before. "Wait," he says. "Was this girl on *Saturday Night Live* a few weeks ago?

"Yes, Rusty, she was. That's Rickie Lee Jones."

"The girl with the beret," says Rusty, recalling the performer's distinctive headwear.

As they continue toward Rusty's house, Carla asks "Any news about Larry?"

Rusty sighs. "No, not really." He decides to tell her of his conversation with Wiseman. After finishing, Rusty asks "Do you think I should say something to him?"

Carla pauses to consider her response. "Well, you could, but I wouldn't expect a miracle. Growing up in Brooklyn, I knew boys like Larry. A couple of them straightened themselves out, but most of them didn't. The ones who do recover have to hit a point where life has become intolerable and they're crying out for help. I don't think Larry's at that point. I'm just glad that he hasn't dragged you down with him. I was really worried about that."

They arrive at the house. Carla stops the car at the end of the driveway. She turns to him and asks softly "You sure you're okay?"

"Yeah, sure," he replies. Then he asks, "You want to come inside and see my house?"

"Sure."

A surge of electricity surges through Rusty as he gets out of her tiny VW Beetle. He leads Carla in through the garage and warns "We have a dog. Don't worry, he's friendly, just a little high-strung." He opens the door to the basement and sure enough Duffy charges over, barking and sneezing in a fury. Rusty reaches down to restrain the dog and prevent him from jumping on Carla.

"Aww...he's so cute!" says Carla, reaching down to pet him.

After calming down the dog, Rusty shows Carla the rec room area of the basement before leading her upstairs, where the kitchen, living room and dining room are. She smiles as she eyes the furnishings.

Now it's time to lead her up the stairs to his bedroom. As he ascends, he is conscious of his heart beating in his chest, and it reminds Rusty of the recent Rod Stewart hit song "Do Ya Think I'm Sexy?" when the singer's heart beats like a drum. He leads Carla to his room. "Sorry it's a mess, I wasn't expecting anyone," he murmurs. Rusty turns to Carla and he can see that she seems nervous. She glances at the corner of his bedroom where keeps his guitars.

"Can you play me something?"

"Sure." He strides over to where his guitars are and selects his acoustic instrument. He sits on his bed and tunes his guitar. Carla sits down next to him, very close by, and Rusty feels a jolt course through his body. He considers what song to play for her. He can now do a pretty good version of Bad Company's "Feel Like Making Love" but decides that it's too dead on. So he settles on another tune that's suited for his voice, The Eagles' "Peaceful Easy Feeling," even though he feels anything but peaceful and easy. Rusty starts off okay, but soon the writer expresses his wish to sleep with his beloved in the desert tonight, so maybe this song is also dead on. He feels himself blush, and he is convinced that Glenn Frey would beat him senseless for butchering his song. But he soldiers on, and when he finishes Carla says, "That was beautiful, Rusty."

Rusty looks at Carla. She is looking at him. He's frozen, not sure if he's supposed to make some kind of move on her. But she solves the problem by leaning over and kissing him. Rusty feels elated, yet also awkward because of the guitar that's perched on his lap. He can't hold her or stroke her hair, so he tries to multitask by removing the guitar as her kisses her. Carla notices, though. She pulls back, and laughing gently she whispers, "You can put it away."

"Okay, thanks." He gets up and puts his guitar back on the stand. Before retaking his spot next to Carla, he turns on the radio behind his bed, and he hears the opening guitar riffs of The Rolling Stones' "Beast of Burden." He returns to Carla and they kiss anew. Now he can stroke her hair and she responds by moaning quietly. Rusty wonders if this is as far as its going to get. Carla's hands, though, are caressing Rusty, first all over his back and then his chest. He in turn strokes her back, then her sides, and then with trepidation, brings his hands to the sides of her breasts. Rusty is expecting her to swat his hands away and scold him, but instead she moans a little louder than before. Rusty feels a surge of excitement, his penis straining against his underwear and blue jeans.

Next, to Rusty's astonishment, she slips her hands underneath his T-shirt and she strokes his back, causing Rusty to shudder and moan. "You're so responsive," says Carla. "I love the feel of your skin, it's so smooth."

"Really?" Rusty asks. He has no idea what his skin feels like to anyone else who might touch it, and until now no girl or woman ever has, other than his mom. Since Carla's hands are under his shirt, he decides he can reciprocate. He lifts up Carla's light sweater and feels her flanks, then upward to her breasts, where he feels the fabric of her brassiere. He waits a few moments then again progresses up to the sides of her breasts.

In one motion, Carla reaches down to the bottom of her sweater and pulls it upward over her head. A wave of arousal goes through Rusty as he beholds Carla's cleavage and the tawny skin of her torso. A new song comes on the radio, and Rusty can hear the opening guitar riffs to "Do Ya Think I'm Sexy?" Rusty lets out an involuntary chuckle.

"What?" asks Carla, smiling.

"It's that song."

Carla listens and laughs. She looks at Rusty and asks, "Do you think I'm sexy?"

"Oh god, yes!"

"Good," she says moving closer. They resume kissing, and Rusty realizes that he ought to remove his T-shirt. He feels embarrassed and self-conscious, and he worries that Carla will be disappointed and worse, turned off. Well, she's seen me run in my cross-country and track uniforms, so she has a general idea of what I look like, he reasons. So, he gently pulls away from Carla and removes his T-shirt. Rusty is rewarded with a smile from Carla. *What does she see in me?*

They resume kissing, and this time Rusty moves his hands all over her breasts. Carla responds to this by moaning softly. Suddenly, she pushes back against Rusty. She brings her arms behind her back. *Oh my god, she isn't!*

Carla unclasps her bra, and ever so slowly allows it to fall on the floor. Rusty briefly remembers a conversation he had last summer with a female cousin who is 18 months his junior. She was mystified by the male obsession with the female breast. "They're just a couple of lumps on your chest," she explained. Rusty had laughed, conceding that she had a point. But as he stares at Carla's large and well-formed breasts, he only knows that some things just can't be explained and that he feels powerless. He doesn't want to get Carla pregnant, but there is no way he can resist her.

Carla, looking directly at Rusty, moves closer. Rusty furtively lifts his hands and gently squeezes and caresses Carla's breasts as they kiss again. After a few moments, Carla pulls back and asks, "Can we lie down for a bit?"

Oh my god!

They lie down on his bed and resume kissing. Carla reaches down and strokes Rusty's groin. He lets out an involuntary gasp before reaching down to do the same. Carla guides his hand to where she wants Rusty to stroke her. Soon she is gasping and occasionally moaning as Rusty apparently touches the right places.

Carla's hand next goes to Rusty's belt buckle and she tries to undo it.

"Need some help?"

"Yes," Carla whispers. Rusty unbuckles his belt, unbuttons his jeans and pulls down the zipper. He has never shown himself to anyone, and he feels a wave of self-consciousness. Carla reaches for Rusty's penis and strokes it. For a moment Rusty thinks he might ejaculate, but then the moment passes. Rusty reaches for Carla's groin. She undoes her pants and pulls them down below her hips.

Rusty caresses Carla before slipping his finger under her panties. He feels her pubic hair, but then Carla grabs his wrist and forces his hand downward to where she wants him to be. He feels much wetness. The things they don't teach you in sex ed, he marvels.

They kiss and feel each other for a couple of minutes. Carla lets go of Rusty, and then tugs at the waistline of his blue jeans. Oh my God, she wants them all the way off! Rusty complies, removing his sneakers, socks, jeans and underwear. When he's finished, he sees that Carla has removed the rest of her clothing.

Until now, Rusty's experience with female nudity was limited to looking at *Playboy* and *Penthouse* magazines with Larry and watching the occasional R-rated film. It's one thing to look at images in a magazine or to watch a nude scene in a movie. It's another thing altogether to see someone he has desired so intensely lying on his own bed. Now, looking at Carla's well-defined abdominal muscles, the dimples on her lower back, her well-toned legs, and of course her breasts, Rusty feels excitement and arousal, but also something else entirely unexpected: fear.

Carla looks at Rusty. "Rusty?"

"Yeah?"

"Are you a virgin?"

"Yeah."

"It's okay," Carla says, reassuringly.

"Carla?"

"Yes?"

"I, I don't want to get you pregnant."

"I'm on the pill, Rusty. But thank you for thinking about that."

They resume kissing and touching. The radio has just started playing Blondie's disco-influenced "Heart of Glass." Rusty tentatively rolls on top of Carla, who spreads her legs to make way for him. He tries to enter her, to no avail at first, but Carla guides him in. At once, he feels himself on the verge of orgasm. Please God, not now, not yet. But it's no use, and Rusty groans and shudders as he ejaculates. He guesses that he was inside her for less than ten seconds. "I'm so sorry, Carla," he gasps.

"That's okay. It happens sometimes with boys during their first time."

"I guess I was too excited." Rusty lies by her side, and they cuddle together, stroking each other's bodies. Rusty has many questions for Carla, but he's too shy and embarrassed to ask.

"What?" asks Carla, almost laughing. She apparently has read his mind, or at least his facial expressions.

"Well, I don't know...I know it's not considered polite to ask a woman this..."

"No, I'm not a virgin!" says Carla.

Rusty laughs sheepishly and feels himself blush. "Well, I kinda figured that. But that wasn't what I was gonna ask you."

"Oh?" she asks, her large eyes wide open.

"I was actually wondering how old you are."

"I'm twenty-four. And I don't mind you asking."

As they lie together, Rusty notices that Carla's eyes are closed, she's smiling, and she occasionally moans softly as he caresses her. Rusty is amazed that Carla is in bed with him in the first place, but even more astonishing is that she's so responsive to his touch. Soon, he feels a stirring in his groin. Rusty's hand moves to her breast, and he caresses it, eliciting a moan from Carla. Rusty quickly becomes erect and his penis touches Carla's hip. She reaches down and feels Rusty. Opening her eyes wide open, she turns to him and says, "Oh my, we don't have much time left, do we?"

They kiss again while the radio begins to play Amii Stewart's disco version of "Knock on Wood." The throbbing beat further arouses Rusty. Once again, he rolls on top of Carla, and again she guides him in. Rusty's erection is firm, but this time he's not on the verge of orgasm, making him more confident.

Rusty's initial thrusts are slow and gentle, though he soon picks up the tempo to match the rhythm of the song. He clutches Carla tighter in his arms, and she shudders and responds in kind. Rusty stares at Carla's face, her eyes are closed, she appears to be in a trance, but the shuddering breaths are more frequent. Rusty moves his head to see more of Carla's body. The sight of his pale frame pressing against her tawny skin arouses him further. Rusty puts his head down, his mouth at Carla's ear, he licks it, and Carla throws her head back against the pillow, arching her neck and moaning all the while. Rusty caresses Carla's arms and shoulders, then her legs and buttocks. He wonders if he can get to her breast. Rusty brings his hand to her rib cage, and turning his body only slightly is able to cup her breast. Carla moans in response and Rusty can feel himself getting firmer as his thrusts get harder and faster. He becomes aware that she is wet down there when she begins yelling, "Oh God, oh God, oh my God, Rusty. I'm coming! Aaaaah!"

For a moment, Rusty feels afraid that he has hurt Carla, and he briefly lets up on his thrusting, but Carla yells "Faster Rusty, faster, harder!" and Rusty resumes his thrusts. The action goes on for about a minute, Rusty is starting to get winded, and he wonders if it's going to happen, but then he feels that sensation. "Oh my God Carla, I'm coming…CARLA!"

After he has finished, he looks down and sees her laughing. "What?" he asks, smiling.

"I think the neighbors know about us," she replies.

"Well, you were kind of loud, too."

Carla adopts a look of mock innocence. "Moi?" She looks at her watch. "Oh my God, it's late! Your mom will be here soon!" She immediately rolls off Rusty's bed and begins to put her clothes on. Rusty, suddenly nervous, follows suit.

He walks Carla to her car. They kiss for a few moments. Rusty says, "I hope we can do this again soon."

Carla smiles. There's a radiance to her that he's never seen before. "Yes, I do, too." She gets into her car and drives off.

Less than five minutes later, his mom arrives home from work.

* * * * *

It's Saturday afternoon. Rusty is bounding along on a trail through a nature preserve that connects his street with Lord's Highway, where he had his bike accident nearly three months ago. He's on his way to meet Carla, who is driving up from Norwalk, where she lives. Earlier, Carla gave Rusty her phone number. She doesn't dare call him. Fortunately, she lives close enough so that it's a local call, and his parents won't see the charges on their phone bill. They have arranged to meet at the end of Lord's Highway, since it's secluded enough so that no one is likely to see him entering her car.

They've decided to see a movie together, so this is Rusty's first actual date with a girl, or in this case a woman. The movie is *Norma Rae*, a film that opened a couple of months ago to rave reviews. The film is playing in Norwalk, not far from Carla's place, and it's safer than seeing it in Westport, where they are more likely to be spotted.

Rusty comes to the end of the trail and stands at the end of Lord's Highway. It feels scary and strange to be sneaking off like this. He doesn't like lying to his parents, but he's desperate to see Carla.

After a few minutes, Rusty hears the approach of a car, and Carla's Volkswagon Beetle appears. He waits until Carla stops at the dead end before hopping in.

"Give me a kiss," Carla commands after Rusty closes the car door. Rusty does what he is told. The kiss is long and passionate. When they finish, Carla asks, "What did you tell your parents?"

"I told them I'm with Larry."

"Does Larry know that?"

"No," Rusty replies.

"What if he calls and asks for you?"

Rusty sighs. "Not much risk of that. He hasn't called in a couple of weeks."

Carla puts the car in gear and they drive off. The music she has on features a man singing in a very high tenor, imploring a girl whose name is Roxanne to turn off her red light.

"This is The Police," Carla announces, with mock sternness.

"What?"

"That's the name of the band," she says, laughing. "They're a group from England. New Wave."

"Oh, okay. That's weird though," says Rusty.

"Why?"

"The guy in the song is in love with a hooker."

* * * * *

Rusty sits with Carla in the cinema, watching *Norma Rae*. Sitting to his right, she leans against him, alternatively holding his hand and stroking his arm. Rusty is of course reciprocating, also occasionally running his fingers through her wavy brown hair.

This alone makes for an intensely erotic experience. Looking at Sally Field on screen adds more to the excitement. His only prior exposure to her was seeing some old *Flying Nun* reruns on television, and some previews of *Sybil*, which he never saw. Until now, he had never thought of her as sexy. Yet now, despite playing a working-class woman in a gritty, grimy low-wage factory job, she manages to look alluring.

* * * * *

Rusty lies in bed with Carla at her place in Norwalk, a duplex that she shares with a female roommate who was in and gave them both a strangely hostile reception. It's a block from a marina and not far from a state park where Rusty and his parents have gone bird watching with the Audubon Society. He once again marvels at the sight of Carla's body as they caress each other. He has read about couples who lose interest in each other, both in fiction and in articles in his mother's women's magazines, and he can't imagine ever losing interest in Carla.

Carla looks at Rusty and smiles. "So, what did you think of the movie?" They both laugh. They hadn't wasted any time in conversation after the movie ended.

"I though it was really good," replies Rusty. After a pause he asks, "Is that what your dad does, what that Reuben guy did?" referring to the Jewish labor organizer from New York who advised Norma Rae.

"Yup, pretty much."

"Wow, that's really admirable. You must be very proud of him."

"I am. It's the one part of my Jewish heritage that I'm most proud of, people trying to make the world a more just place."

"Is that also why you decided to become a teacher? To give back to the world, in a way?"

"Yeah, I'd say that's part of it."

"You know, I've heard that you're a great teacher. One of my talent show bandmates is in one of your classes. She loves you as a teacher! I'd love to take one of your classes someday."

"You'd better not!"

Rusty senses he has said something very wrong. "What do you mean?"

"Rusty, if you become a student of mine, I'll have to break up with you. I mean that. I have to be objective when I grade people's work, and I can't be if you are my lover. For god's sake, Rusty, please don't!"

She's on the verge of tears, and this shocks Rusty, since he's never seen her so emotional before. "I promise I'll never do that."

"Oh, Rusty," she says, reaching over to him and burying her face into his chest. "I don't want to lose you, ever!"

Rusty holds her tight, and they lie there like this for a few minutes. He remains shocked. He's still amazed that he's in bed with Carla, but what's happening now? Is she in love with him?

Suddenly Carla looks up at Rusty. "You have to be home soon, don't you?"

"Yeah, by dinner time."

"What time is that?"

"6:30."

"Oh my! We have to get going!"

Reluctantly, Rusty gets up and puts on his clothes. Even spending the night with Carla would not be enough. Rusty thinks, I want to spend the rest of my life with her.

* * * * *

It's raining today, so track practice is being held indoors. This is depressing for Rusty since the spring season is supposed to liberate one from having to do running workouts on the hard hallway surface. Rusty wanted to run outside anyway on the streets, if not on the cinder track surface, which is not allowed when it's raining. He had no takers from any of his teammates; nobody wanted to run in the rain. So, after the stretching routines, Rusty resigns himself to the inevitable.

Rusty looks around. Once again, no Larry. He's pretty much blown off most of the season. He's been acting strange lately, during the rare times he's shown up for school, becoming uncharacteristically quiet and withdrawn, and this alarms Rusty most of all.

He casts a glance at Carla, who is standing with Coach Scarpella. She's been discreet during this past week or so, scarcely acknowledging Rusty until his track workout is done, when she waits for him to emerge from the boys' locker room, before she takes him back to his house where they make love. Norwalk is too far away for them to get things done before his mom comes home on weekdays.

Rusty and his teammates begin to run a couple of easy warmup laps before they begin their main workout, 6 x 330s. They run past the cafeteria, the faculty office, Rusty's locker, before they make the left turn into the smoking lounge area, and there's Larry standing impassively, clad in his black leather jacket and blue jeans. "Larry, what the fuck?" asks Rusty, gesturing his astonishment with raised arms. Larry smiles slightly and shrugs.

"Have a nice workout."

Have a nice workout? He considers stopping and confronting Larry but decides against it. When Rusty passes through the smoking lounge for a second time, Larry's gone.

* * * * *

The next morning, Rusty is in Mr. Consalvo's English class for his first period. He is feeling quite satisfied, for he has just turned in his sophomore paper at the beginning of class, a full week before it was due...because of Carla's help. Carla, his lover. He still can't believe she is actually his girlfriend.

His reverie is interrupted by the high school intercom. He hears a voice say, "May I have your attention. This is Mr. Hessman, your principal. I'm afraid that I have to convey some tragic news to you all. Larry Furillo, a student here at Northfield, died yesterday afternoon."

"What?" gasps Rusty out loud, jerking upright in his chair.

"It further pains me to inform you that his death was the result of suicide..."

No, this can't be! I just saw him yesterday... Rusty immediately stands up and bolts from the classroom. He dashes out to the hallway and runs toward the smoking lounge, where he last saw Larry. A part of him knows this is futile, he's not going to find him. Yet the part of him that holds on to a shred a hope drives him forward.

"Rusty!" It's Carla's voice. She has somehow found Rusty and is pursuing him. She catches up to him. "Rusty, I'm so sorry..."

"He was here!" Rusty says in disbelief.

"What do you mean?"

"He was right there!" he says, jabbing his finger in the direction of the smoking lounge. "I saw him there during practice. We talked a little."

"That was yesterday afternoon, Rusty. He died last night."

"How the hell did he do it?" Rusty asks.

"Carbon monoxide poisoning. He locked the car in the garage and turned on the ignition. The rest of the family was away."

"Oh, god, oh fuck, oh my fucking god!" Rusty exclaims, his face buried in his hands.

"Come on, Rusty, lets get away from here. We'll go to your guidance counselor's office." She puts her arm around Rusty's waist and leads him back in the direction of the staff offices. Stunned students in the hallway look on as they walk past, but they barely register in Rusty's mind. When they arrive at the guidance counselor's office, Carla pushes Rusty into a chair. "I think you should go home. Why don't I call your mom? Do you have her work number?" Rusty nods. She finds a slip of paper and Rusty jots it down. Carla goes off to find a phone, and Rusty realizes that his secret flame is going to be speaking to his mom. This unsettles him even more. Within few minutes, Carla returns.

"I spoke to your mom, she's on her way. I have to teach another class, and I'm late. I'm so sorry, Rusty!" She reaches down to Rusty and gives him a platonic hug. Through his curtain of grief, he feels an erotic surge.

"Thank you," Rusty manages to gasp as he starts to weep. The enormity of this tragedy has finally sunk in.

His mother arrives about twenty minutes later. She appears almost as shocked as Rusty feels, and she immediately embraces him. "Oh, Peter, why would he do this?"

"I don't know."

They turn and leave the office. As they walk slowly down the hallway toward the front door she remarks "I must say, this Ms. Levy is a very nice young woman. She really seems to care about you."

* * * * *

Rusty stands forlornly in line with his parents at Larry's wake. He feels strange in the formal clothes he's wearing, particularly the tie that his father had to help put on. He looks at the long queue of people in front and behind him, recognizing many teammates and classmates with parents in tow, like Rusty. There are plenty of others who Rusty doesn't recognize, presumably friends of Larry's family. They eventually enter the funeral home, a Victorian-era structure, whose interior is decorated with Christian symbols and paintings, mainly of the crucifixion and ascension. He can see Larry's family receiving the well-wishers. There is Mr. Furillo, a tall, beefy former college football player and javelin thrower turned businessman. There is Larry's mom, the tall, slender, elegant blond who had been a professional model before marriage and motherhood. Finally, there is Frances, Larry's kid sister, a pig-tailed sixth grader.

All three of his surviving family appear to be holding it all together but barely, especially Frances. Rusty wonders how the hell could Larry do this to them. Rusty's mother, a devout Catholic, once told Rusty that suicide is a mortal sin, since it's taking a life, even if it's your own.

They finally reach the family. Rusty has no idea about what to say to them. He faces Larry's mom. Her eyes are damp and bloodshot, yet she looks at him with an expression of compassion. "Oh, Rusty, thank you for coming!"

"Mrs. Furillo...I'm so sorry," he gasps before dissolving into tears. Mrs. Furillo reaches over to Rusty and embraces him.

"You were such a good friend to him. I'm so glad you were a part of his life."

After leaving the family, Rusty heads to the casket to see his friend for the final time. Like Rusty, Larry is wearing a suit and tie, and it's discomfiting to see him like this. He finds it hard to believe it's really him. As per custom, Rusty kneels before him, as if in prayer, but what sort of prayer can he say for him, really? His embalmed, wax museum-like remains are there, but Rusty doesn't feel his presence. Instead, he feels numb. So, he stands up and heads over to a group of teammates who are gathered nearby. They immediately embrace Rusty and convey their sympathies. Michael Wiseman asks, "How you holding up, Raz?"

"I don't know, man, I can't believe this happened."

"Yeah, I know," says Wiseman, turning to look at Larry. "You know, I just want to go up to him and say, 'Okay Larry, we got the joke, you had us fooled, you can get up now.' A part of me believes that would actually happen."

"Yeah, if only." Rusty turns away to look at the others in the room. Carla has entered, in a black dress. She makes her way down, introducing herself to Larry's family. Carla was never a big fan of Larry's, and she wasn't at all secretive about it with Rusty. Yet here she is. She proceeds to Larry's coffin, looks at him and quickly turns away, appearing shaken. Carla sees Rusty and walks right over to him.

"Oh, Rusty, how are you doing?" Rusty can't make a verbal reply. He just throws up his hands. "I know Rusty, I know." Carla casts a furtive glance in another direction before looking again at Rusty. "I love you," she says in a whisper.

It is then that Wiseman approaches Carla and says, "Ms. Levy, good to see you."

Rusty looks in the direction Carla had been glancing at. He sees his parents, his mom chatting away with other parents, his father staring in Carla's direction. She is talking to Wiseman but standing close to Rusty.

He realizes that Carla came here because of him.

* * * * *

Rusty sits in his U.S. history class, listening as Mrs. Lewis discusses America's entry into World War II. A tall spindly woman, she has an enthusiastic way of lecturing. This is a help, for Rusty has been a cauldron of emotions since Larry's death. He's also distracted by thoughts of Carla. She wasn't at school yesterday or today, and a sub has taken over for her.

Is she sick?

He hears a knock on the classroom door. It opens, and there stands Mr. Hessman, the high school principal. He motions Mrs. Lewis toward him. Rusty can hear Mr. Hessman say, "Sorry to disturb your class," before his voice trails off to an inaudible level. He notices Mr. Hessman gesturing in Rusty's direction, and he tenses up. After a few seconds he says "Peter, I need you to come with me."

Stunned, Rusty stands up and grabs his notebook and textbook. "May I ask what this is about?"

"Let's wait until we get to my office. I'll explain it then."

Rusty becomes extremely alarmed as he considers the possibilities. Getting pulled out of class by the principal generally involves something pretty bad.

They arrive at the principal's office, where a large bald man with a brush mustache awaits. The man looks familiar to Rusty, and he soon remembers seeing his picture in the local paper. It's Joe Stetler, the Northfield Police Department's detective. Mr. Hessman says "Joe, this is Peter Rassmussen, the student I told you about."

The detective smiles. "Hi, Peter, why don't we step inside and have a chat." Peter is led into Mr. Hessman's office. The principal closes the door behind Rusty, leaving him alone with the detective. He motions Rusty to have a seat. Stetler begins by saying "First of all, I want you to know that you're not in any trouble, and I want to reassure you of that."

A silence ensues, with Stetler clearly awaiting a response from Rusty. "Okay."

"Can you tell me something about your relationship with Ms. Levy, the English teacher?"

Oh fuck! So, this is what it's about. How the fuck did anybody find out? Rusty suddenly feels both nauseous and short of breath. Detective Stetler is staring right at him, and Rusty wonders if his own facial expressions and body language are giving everything away. "Well...I know her."

"We know that you know her, Peter," Stetler replies. "The question is how well you know her. Can you tell me about your relationship with her?" He thinks about what Travis had said to him. Whatever you do Rusty, don't admit anything.

"I don't know...she's someone I've known since she first started teaching here, that's all."

"How old are you, Peter?"

"I'm sixteen."

"And how old were you when you first met her?"

"Fifteen."

"Have you had her for any of your classes?"

"No sir."

"Never taken a class with her?"

"No."

"So how do you know her?"

"She coaches the girls' cross-country and track teams. I'm on the boys' team."

"Are you close to her?" Stetley asks.

Rusty senses a trap looming. He asks, "What's this about?" in a tone sharper than he intended.

The detective pauses before saying "I'm here to investigate an allegation that she had an inappropriate relationship with you."

"What do you mean? Like I slept with her or something?"

Stetler nods his head.

"Well, that's bullshit."

"Look, I know you are trying to stand up for her, and I think that's admirable, but you don't have much to worry about. If you didn't or don't have her for a class, then she wasn't or isn't in a position of authority over you. The age of consent here in Connecticut is 16, so as long as you weren't intimate with her before your 16th birthday, she's not in any legal jeopardy."

Rusty's nausea gets worse. *This guy's mindfucking me.* "Sir, I already told you that's bullshit. Who told you I was having an affair with her?"

"What if I was to say she told me that?"

Rusty feels a yet another shock in his system. At first, he has no idea how to respond. *Whatever you do, don't admit anything!* "Then you bring her up here and have her say that to my face!"

Stetler continues to stare at Rusty impassively. It's obvious to Rusty that the detective is believing none of it. Finally, the detective takes a breath, lets out a wan smile and says, "Okay, Peter, that'll do for now. I'm going to have a word with Mr. Hessman, and I'll be on my way."

Stetler stands and heads for the door. Once outside, the two men have a brief talk before Mr. Hessman walks in and says, "Peter, could you wait outside my office, please?"

Rusty takes a seat outside the office as the door closes and the two men confer inside. He's in shock, paralyzed by fear for himself and Carla. How the fuck did anybody find out about this, he wonders again. He hadn't said anything to anyone about it. And did Carla confess, or was the detective lying, the way they do in the movies?

The door to the office opens, Mr. Stetler leaves, and Mr. Hessman says, "Peter, come inside, and shut the door."

Rusty takes a deep breath, stands up and walks into the office. Mr. Hessman is a tall, burly man of about forty. He is fairly new here, having only started as principal this past September. He has adopted a hands-on, new sheriff in town approach to his job. For example, he would occasionally barge into both the boys' and girls' bathrooms to roust out students who were smoking. Rusty has only met Mr. Hessman briefly. He has no idea what he's in for.

"Come on in, Peter, sit down," he says, gesturing toward the chair in front of his desk. "I spoke with Detective Stetler, and he filled me in on what you told him." Mr. Hessman leans forward, staring intently at Rusty. "Peter, is there something you want to say to me? Something you want to get off your chest?"

Rusty stirs in his seat. "Um...no," he says, shaking his head.

"You realize, Peter, that I take these allegations very seriously. I know this was a shock to you, having to talk to a policeman, but it was something that had to be done."

"Who made these accusations?" asks Rusty, his tone a bit sharper than he intended.

"I can't go into that, Peter."

"What's going to happen to Carla...I mean Ms. Levy?" Rusty winces at his mistake.

"She has resigned her position."

Rusty feels a stabbing sensation. "What? Why? I mean, nothing happened. Are you saying she left her job because of me?"

"Peter, I don't want you to think of it that way. Look, I know you've been through a lot lately, and I feel bad about that. You lost your best friend, and before that you had a bike accident. Feel free to see your guidance counselor if you need to talk to someone. Ms. Levy will be fine. She's a bright and intelligent woman with a great future. Anyway, I think you should go home now and think it over. If you want to stop by and talk, we can certainly arrange that."

Rusty realizes that he's gotten all the information that he can get from Mr. Hessman. Someone obviously tipped him off. Rusty had kept his secret, so either Carla said something to somebody, or someone had seen them together and ratted them out. There's no other possibility.

Rusty emerges from the principal's office feeling shell-shocked. Oh god, first Larry and now this. He staggers out to the empty hallway. He's not sure where to go.

"Hey, Raz!"

Startled, he looks around. It's Wiseman, the team captain. He asks, "Are you all right?"

Rusty only nods.

Wiseman appears unconvinced. "Coach wants to talk to you."

"Okay," Rusty mumbles. *Oh god, forget the cop and the principal, I'm really dead now. He's fucking pissed. He's going to tear my head off for sure.* Rusty considers avoiding the coach, but soon concludes that if Scarpella really wants to talk, he will hunt Rusty down. Better to come to him. So he shuffles down the hallway toward the locker room. Along the way, he passes by kids who give him sideways glances, and others who stare right at him. Great, Rusty thinks. I'm the talk of the whole student body, freshmen to senior class. I lost my best friend to suicide, and now everyone knows about my affair with Carla. That's all they're talking about now.

Rusty enters the locker room and peeks through the large window into the coach's office. Scarpella is seated at his desk, talking with Coach Best, the burly gym teacher and assistant football coach. The two seem to be having a pleasant conversation, both smiling and laughing until Scarpella spots Rusty. Scarpella turns to Best and jerks his head toward the door. Best, taking his cue, smiles and waves to Scarpella before turning toward the door. Upon crossing the threshold, Best gives Rusty a sideways glance, his smile gone. Even the faculty, too.

Rusty appears at the door. "Come in, close the door and have a seat," Scarpella says, gesturing to a chair in front of his desk. Rusty does as he is told, feeling a constriction in his chest. But something unexpected is happening. Scarpella is looking at Rusty with an expression that appears to be of genuine concern.

"How ya doin, Rusty?" he asks quietly.

Rusty isn't sure how to respond. He mumbles "Okay, I guess."

"Yeah?"

Rusty looks down. Here it comes.

"First of all, I want to tell you how sorry I am about Larry. I know he was your friend. I tried talking some sense into him, but I never got through. I failed, and it hurts because I was just like him when I was your age. No, I was worse. I was far worse. I was a punk kid, getting into fights, stealing cars, you name it. The Marines straightened me out. I learned discipline there, and it made me the man I am today. Anyway, I wish I could have talked some sense into him, but I couldn't. I'm sorry."

A long uncomfortable pause ensues. Then Scarpella says, "There's something else I want to bring up."

Uh-oh. "Okay," says Rusty with trepidation.

"I was wondering if you could do me a favor."

Now Rusty is confused. "Okay," he says again.

"The WCCs are tomorrow. We got a tough, tough track meet ahead of us. I could use you in the 880."

"Okay, yeah, sure, I'll run it," replies Rusty.

"I know you've missed some days with what's been going on."

"Actually, I've managed to get some running in."

"Yeah?" says the coach, smiling.

"Yeah, nothing major. Been doing five milers, with some strides thrown in, no biggie."

"Really? Good!" replies his coach.

For a change, Rusty is telling somebody the truth, and it feels good. He has been running. For Rusty, running and playing the guitar are times of solace, the only times in his day when life makes any sense.

"Go get yourself suited up. Go easy, just do some light jogging. We got a big day tomorrow."

"Okay, coach," Rusty replies. He stands up, heads back into the locker room. Taking a deep breath, he lets out a sigh of relief that lasts for eternity.

* * * * *

Rusty slowly walks down his street on his way home after his short pre-race workout. This time he was able to catch the late bus, which deposited him at a spot about a quarter mile from his house. He's not looking forward to coming home, since he's anticipating a confrontation with his mother. She would likely have returned home early from work if she heard anything about it from school. Rusty is not sure what he's going to say, but he knows it won't be the truth. His mom is a devout Roman Catholic. Sex before marriage is a mortal sin, particularly if it involves a teacher. The fact that she's unmarried and he hasn't sinned against the commandment involving adultery would make it only marginally better. She wouldn't be able to handle it, and Rusty wouldn't be able to bear her reaction.

Sure enough, her car is parked in the garage. He enters the house via the garage and into the basement. Once again, his dog Duffy charges over to greet him. Rusty sinks to his knees to pet him, and he ends up holding him tightly, like a shipwreck survivor holding onto a piece of floating debris.

Rusty enters the kitchen, and his sister Patti intercepts him. A slim, pale-skinned blonde woman of medium height, she is subletting her Manhattan apartment and is staying here for a few days before heading down to Cincinnati, where she has an acting job in summer stock.

"Rusty, you're in the doghouse!" she warns.

"Yeah?"

"Our mother has heard from the school. Something about you having an affair with a teacher."

"Well, it didn't happen, Patti."

Patti doesn't look remotely convinced.

"Where is she?" Rusty asks in resignation.

"She's in the family room. Good luck."

Rusty walks into the family room and finds his mother sitting stone faced on a rocking chair, a magazine on her lap. "Hi, Mom," he says quietly.

"Sit down, Peter," she commands. Rusty takes a seat across from her.

"I got a phone call from the principal today. He told me about an inappropriate relationship you had with Ms. Levy."

"It's not true, mom."

"Don't lie to me, Peter! How could you do such an immoral thing?"

Immoral? He wants to ask, since when is being in love immoral? Unfortunately, since he's lying to his mother about the existence of this affair, he's unable to go down that path.

"Mom, I don't know who said what to who, I don't know why anyone would accuse her of anything. I was friends with her, yes. We talked about things, you know, books, movies, stuff like that. But we weren't anything like...that. Hell, you saw her with that guy after we saw *The Deer Hunter*.

She was on a date! He was an adult, right? Why would she go out with someone like me? I'm just a kid!"

His mother looks down and away. She appears to be on the verge of bursting into tears. "I want to believe you, Peter."

"Mom, I don't know what more I can say." His voice is quavering. "My life is a train wreck. I mean, first Larry, and now this? Really Mom, I don't know how much more can I take!"

His mom closes her eyes as a tears moves down her cheek. "It's okay, Peter. I'm sorry. I believe you now."

Rusty winces at that, though his mother doesn't see it. For now, he has this on his conscience as well: he has lied to his mother.

After this, Rusty flees upstairs to his bedroom. He flings himself onto the bed, buries his face into a pillow, and pounds his fists against the mattress.

* * * * *

Rusty stands on the New Fairfield High School track with seven other runners, awaiting the start of the boys 880-yard run at the WCC track and field championships. He isn't sure that he really belongs in this race, having missed several practices and the state qualifying meet. What he does know for certain is that this will be the last 880-yard race he will ever run.

Rusty isn't planning to quit the track team, nor is he switching events. Rather, it's because two weeks ago Coach Scarpella announced to his surprised teammates that effective January 1, 1980, all high school cross-country and track races in Connecticut will be run in metric distances. All cross-country races will be run in the standard 5K distance. Next year, Rusty will run the 1000 meters in indoor track, a longer distance than 1000 yards, and in outdoor track the 800 meters, a slightly shorter distance than 880 yards.

Upon hearing the news, Rusty thought: Connecticut, and all of America, is finally catching up to the rest of the world! He imagines a future adulthood where he and his fellow Americans will weigh themselves in kilos instead of pounds, where the weather forecaster will announce the current temperature in Celcius degrees instead of Fahrenheit, and the speed limit signs will be in kilometers per hour.

"Hey, Rassmussen, what's up?" Rusty turns, and sees it's Trevor Lavelle, his shaggy blond hair blowing in the soft breeze.

"Not much," Rusty replies. Actually, there's a lot going on with me, Rusty thinks. Should I tell him about my affair with Carla or my best friend's suicide?

"I heard you guys lost someone," Trevor says.

"Yeah, we did."

"Do I know him?" Trevor asks.

"He was a miler. Dark-haired guy, built more like a football player than a runner."

Trevor's blue eyes open wide. "Was he the guy I saw you hang out with?"

Rusty looks down. He is unable to look at Trevor at this point. "Yeah," he says quietly.

"Oh, fuck man, I'm so sorry." There is an awkward silence, and Rusty senses that Trevor is unsure what to say next. Please don't ask me how he died. Finally, he says "You take care, man. Good luck in the race."

"Thanks," replies Rusty. "You too." Well, thinks Rusty, not only is this Trevor a fast runner, he seems to be a decent guy as well.

Rusty and Trevor jog in place to stay warmed up. The track, unlike Norfield's, is an "all weather" track, a hard rubber surface. Rusty feels strong, and the weather is rather cool for a late May afternoon, ideal for running. Maybe I'll do okay, Rusty thinks. No way I'll beat Trevor, but maybe I'll get a PR and score some points for the team.

"Okay, runners to the starting line," an official orders. Rusty and the other runners walk or jog to the starting line. He feels a pinching sensation in his insides, probably pre-race nerves,.

"Runners on your mark!" Rusty and his competitors crouch and place their lead foot on the line. "Stead-EEE!" the starter screams. Despite his inner angst, Rusty has to stifle a chuckle.

The gun goes off, and Rusty settles behind the others in dead last place, but right behind the runner in front of him. The pack of runners in front of him appear to be tightly bunched, though he can see Trevor surging ahead. They come to the first straight, and the pack begins to stretch out. Rusty remains last, keeping the next runner close. The pace feels comfortable, sustainable so far.

They come to the second turn, and thoughts of Carla and Larry come to mind. The pain and the sorrow return. Rusty wants to do something, surge ahead of some people, but he restrains himself. Coming to the second straightaway he hears the voices of his teammates cheering him on. Approaching the end of the first lap, Rusty hears a man call out the splits. "Fifty Five, Fifty Six, Fifty Seven." Rusty sees Trevor cross the line at "Fifty Eight!" Seconds later, Rusty crosses at 1:03.

On the first curve again, thoughts of Carla and Larry resurface. To distract himself, he remembers being nine years old, watching the '72 Olympics on a black and white TV because his father was too frugal to buy a color TV, and seeing Dave Wottle, the man with the goofy golf cap, make that incredible surge from dead last over the final 300 meters to steal the gold medal. It seems to Rusty to be an impossible feat to replicate here. He approaches the end of the curve. He thinks of Carla.

Now!

One by one, Rusty surges past runners in rapid succession on the back stretch. As he approaches the final curve, he settles behind a runner wearing the maroon singlet of Bethel High. There are three runners head of Rusty, Lavelle is at least thirty yards ahead. Rusty feels a bit ragged, he's definitely breathing heavier due to running at a much faster pace, but he feels strong enough to mount a final charge. He thinks of Wottle's final sprint in Munich. Next, he sees Larry lying in his casket, and now that he's approaching the final stretch, he thinks of Carla.

Now!

On the final stretch, Rusty surges past the runner from Bethel, and he gains on a runner from Brookfield. About 60 yards from the finish, he passes him, too. Lavelle is twenty feet ahead, there's no way I'm catching him, he thinks. I'm running out of real estate, and I'm running out of air. But he's gaining on Lavelle with each step, moving to fifteen feet, then ten feet behind. Twenty yards from the finish, he can see Coach Scarpella in a crouched position, a stopwatch in his hand, his face red, tendons bulging out of his neck. "Hussle, Rassmussen, hussle! You got him!" *No, I fucking don't*, he thinks, but now he's five feet behind Lavelle, and with ten yards to go he thinks...

CARLA!

With a final push, he surges past Lavelle and sails through the finish line. His legs however, having been completely deprived of oxygen, collapse under him, and he falls limply onto the track.

Rusty lies prone on the track's surface, his mouth wide open, sucking in air like a victim of a near drowning. He hears Coach Scarpella ask, "Rusty, are you alright?"

"Yeah," he gasps.

"Good, let's get you up."

Rusty takes the hand of his coach, and with much effort stands up, his legs quivering like those of a newborn colt. He finds himself facing Lavelle. "Hell of a race Raz. Great job, you got me this time."

"Thanks Trev," Rusty replies. He really is a good kid.

Rusty's time is 1:59.2, a new school record. Because of the upcoming change to metric distances, Rusty will go to his grave being the only runner from Northfield High to run a half mile in under two minutes.

JUNE 1979

It's a hot and sultry Saturday afternoon, and Rusty is riding his bike at a furious pace toward Norwalk, desperate to see Carla again, or at least to get some information about her. He has a feeling that the former scenario is unlikely. Rusty has called Carla and got a message that her phone was disconnected. She probably moved out of her apartment. Still, he wants information about her, anything.

Rusty's victory in that race, while just a few days past, feels like a distant memory. Even his grief over Larry's death, profound as it is, has taken a back seat. All thoughts lead to Carla.

He has never ridden his bike this far before, and once he gets to Norwalk, he discovers that riding in city streets is disconcerting. Adding to the tension is the fact that Rusty doesn't know exactly where Carla's apartment is. Using his parent's Hagstrom Fairfield County atlas, he was able to plot a route to the general area where her neighborhood was. He also is aided by his vivid recollections of that date.

Rusty finds the road that leads to a state park that he remembers from his childhood. He remembers that her apartment was on a side street to his right. The question is, which one? He tries one street, then another. No dice. Rusty proceeds to the third street, turns right, and bingo! This is it. He remembers the neighboring houses, what they looked like. Rusty looks to his left and finds Carla's place. Rusty turns into the driveway and rides to the small tenants' parking area in back. Carla's VW is not there. Undeterred, Rusty turns around and heads back to the front.

Rusty parks his bike and, after looking around, decides to lock his bike—just to be safe. With trepidation, he walks to the front door, his legs rubbery from the long ride. Taking a deep breath, he knocks.

Withing seconds, Rusty hears the sound of locks disengaging. The door opens, and a short, frumpily dressed young woman scowls at him. "What do you want?" she growls.

"Is Carla here?"

"No!"

Rusty is taken aback by her rudeness. There was something about her that put him off the first time he was here. Her response confirms his initial feelings. Still, he feels the need to press her.

"Do you know where she is?"

"She moved out of here a couple of weeks ago."

"Do you know where she's living now?"

"How the hell should I know that? Now get lost!" She slams the door hard, nearly hitting Rusty's nose.

Rusty stands stunned for a few seconds before an overwhelming rage takes hold. He slams his fist hard against the door. "Bitch!" he shouts. Rusty heads back to his bike. Once he unlocks it, he decides to head to the end of the street, where he sees boats docked in a marina. He has a long ride back home, and he'll have to leave soon if he wants to get home in time for dinner, but he needs to stop and think. He parks his bike and sits at the edge of the marina, burying his face in his hands.

I've got to find her somehow.

* * * *

The next day, Rusty is headed to Travis's place. He has not been there since Larry's death. His father is silent as he drives. Rusty senses that his parents don't know what to say to him. His mom occasionally asks him if he's okay. Rusty tells her that he is, but he feels she's not buying that.

His father pulls into Travis's driveway. Rusty gets out, and as he retrieves his guitar from the back, he hears his father say, "See you in an hour."

Rusty approaches the door and rings the doorbell. Almost immediately, Travis opens the door. "Whoa, what happened to you?"

"That fucking obvious?"

"Uh, yeah. Come on in buddy. Talk to me, what's going on? Haven't seen you in a while."

"Where do I begin?" Rusty nonetheless tells Travis everything about his unraveling life, including Larry's death and wake, as well as the affair with Carla and its aftermath. After he finishes, Travis is left stunned.

"So you never told anyone else about Carla?"

"No."

"Well, someone sure as shit ratted her out." He shakes his head and looks at Rusty. "I'm sorry this happened to you, buddy. Has Carla gotten in touch with you since she left?"

"No, she hasn't."

"Well, I hope she does. It would be kind of wrong for her not to." After a pause, Travis says, "I know that you're not in a state of mind to focus on the guitar right now. I'd thought I'd offer you a little something else that might help. But you can't tell your folks I'm doing this."

"What's that?"

"Just a minute, you'll see."

Travis disappears into another room. Rusty can't imagine anything that can rescue him from this immense and never-ending anguish that he's been feeling. Travis re-emerges, holding a small white object in his fingers. Rusty squints and asks, "What's that?"

"That, my friend, is a joint, as in marijuana, ganja, reefer, weed: pick your name. Wanna try it?"

"Yeah, okay."

Travis fishes out a lighter from his pants pocket and sits across from Rusty. He places the joint between his lips and lights it. He takes a pull from the joint and then hands it over to Rusty, who takes it with trepidation and a sense of guilt, though he's not sure why. He puts it to his lips and sucks inward.

Instantly, the smoke he's inhaled irritates his throat, so that he sputters and coughs. "Holy smokes!" he gasps between coughs.

"Go easier on it," advises Travis. He demonstrates with his face and hand. "Like this."

Rusty does as he's told. The next hit is taken with far less coughing. His head feels hazy, and he feels calmer, far less sad and distraught. He hands the joint back to Travis. "Thanks."

"No problemo."

Rusty leans back in his seat and stares out a window. He enjoys the hazy feeling.

"Anyway," Travis continues, "I hope this makes you feel better. I'm sorry about what happened, but you'll be all right. You're a good-looking kid. You'll find another girl."

Rusty continues to look out a window. "Yeah, maybe. I just can't imagine finding anyone who sends me like she does."

* * * * *

Rusty sits at his desk in his bedroom, trying to focus on the textbook in front of him. Final exams are coming up. After he's done with his finals, he and his mom will make the annual drive to the Chicago area, where they will stay with his Uncle Harry and Aunt Peggy, who is his mother's sister. They have six children, and two of his cousins are close enough to Rusty's age to be good companions. After returning from that, he'll be taking a driver's ed course. His father has already had him behind the wheel of their Ford Torino station wagon instead of the Ford Pinto, because the Torino has automatic transmission, and he has Rusty drive on residential streets that are not too busy.

Rusty knows he should be excited about the upcoming summer and being able to eventually drive a car. He should be feeling elated if not merely satisfied about his win at the league championships and setting a school record.

Instead, he continues to grieve over Larry's death and losing Carla. With Larry, Rusty alternates between feelings of guilt and rage. The guilt comes from feeling that there was something he might have done or said to prevent his suicide. There are other times, though, when anger overcomes Rusty, resulting in uncharacteristic outbursts. During one, he cried out to his mother, saying "I just wonder sometimes, if he ever just once before he did this, ever consider what this would fucking do to his family and friends like me?"

His mother, normally not one to tolerate foul language, didn't reprimand Rusty. "I don't know Rusty," she admitted sadly. "I just don't know what he was thinking or why he would do this."

A few days later, Rusty talked about it with Travis, the only person in Rusty's life who knows everything that's happening to him. After hearing Rusty pour out his feelings, Travis leaned back and said, "You know, Rusty, I once went through a bad spell, after I got fired from a band I had been playing with, and my wife left me for some other guy. I thought about ending it all. I know that on the surface, suicide seems to be the most selfish and cowardly thing you can do. But it ain't. It comes from a helplessness, a feeling that you're totally fucked, and that life ain't ever gonna get any better. I'm sure your buddy would rather have been alive and hanging out with you."

And then there's Carla. He continues to feel stung by the reception he got from her roommate. Rusty can't stop thinking about Carla. He wonders if she's okay, where she is, what she plans to do next with her life. Above all, he desperately wants her back.

He has been unable to focus on his studies, and he worries that his grades will suffer. At least he got an A on his sophomore paper. Rusty wants to thank Carla for her help. He knows he couldn't have done it without her.

Rusty hears a soft knock on his bedroom door. "Come in," he says.

Rusty's father enters. He has a grave and reproachful look on his face, his Nordic blue eyes casting a blank stare that seems to last forever. He stands before him silent for a few awkward seconds, and Rusty begins to worry. *What did I do now?*

"You got a letter in the mail," he says finally. He hands Rusty an envelope. Rusty takes it and looks. It is indeed addressed to Rusty, but there is no return address. The postmark is from New York City. Nonetheless, he instantly recognizes the handwriting. It's from Carla.

Rusty looks up at his father, whose facial expression hasn't changed a bit. A few more seconds of uncomfortable silence ensue. Finally, he says, "Your mother will be calling you down for supper soon." He turns and walks away.

Rusty stares at his dad as he leaves the room. He knows. *He fucking knows! Don't ask me how, but he knows that I had an affair with Carla. He's not confronting me with this, though. Why? Well, Dad is not a man who's into confrontation. He also might be afraid that I would confess if confronted. I have no intention of confessing, ever, but he doesn't know that. If I did confess, he would then be faced with an awful choice. Either say nothing to Mom, and thus keep a secret from the woman he loves or tell her and watch it all come apart. So, he's going to let this sleeping dog lie and hope it all goes away by itself.*

Good thing he's the one who checked the mail.

Rusty carefully opens the envelope, fighting the urge to rip it open. A photo falls out onto his desk. It's a beautiful black and white head shot of her. With both extreme dread and anticipation, he opens the letter and begins to read.

My dearest Rusty,

I've been so conflicted about writing you this letter. I don't want it to fall into the wrong hands and get you into more trouble, and I know that's the last thing you need. But I couldn't leave my job without saying anything to you.

It breaks my heart to say this, but I can't see you anymore. I know you will find another girl who sees the wonderful qualities that I see in you.

"No, NO!" moans Rusty aloud. He buries his face in his hands and begins to sob. It's just too much. Larry's death, and now losing Carla, it's just too much to bear. Trying to rub his eyes dry, Rusty forces himself to read the letter to the end.

I feel that I've lost the most profound and wonderful love of my life! I'm no longer living in Norwalk, so please don't look for me there. Please know that I really do love you, and that I'll always hope you find love and happiness.
Love, Carla.

"Rusty? Dinner!" he hears his mother call out from downstairs.

Oh, God, this is trouble. He is sobbing uncontrollably, and if his parents see him like this, they're going to ask questions, and with good reason. He's got to get himself together pronto. First, he opens a drawer in his desk, and jams the letter, envelope and photo inside and shuts it. He rubs his eyes and takes deep breaths in a desperate effort to stop weeping.

"Rusty?" his mother calls again, her tone louder and more strident.

"Coming!" he yelps. A final wipe of the eyes and he heads downstairs.

He enters the kitchen looking downward. His mother says, "Rusty, can you turn off the TV?"

"Sure," he replies. He walks to the family room, where the TV is blaring. It's on Channel 2, the local news is on. Some atmospheric disturbance is wreaking havoc with the picture, the images devolving into distorted figures like that of a funhouse mirror. Nonetheless, he can follow the news story. A six-year-old boy in New York City had disappeared while on his way to school some time ago, just vanished from the face of the earth. Police and neighbors have canvassed the city and found nothing. Rusty senses that this is not going to end well. He also wonders why anyone would want to live in New York. His sister has only lived there for a year and a half, before subletting her apartment. She was once held up at gunpoint at the cheese store where she worked and mugged at knifepoint on the street one evening. Yeah, sure, she's an aspiring actress, and if you're trying to make it in showbiz, New York is the place to be. Still, with all that crime, is it really worth it? No fucking way am I living there, Rusty concludes.

Rusty turns off the TV and heads back to the kitchen, where he sits down at the table. His mother has already dished out the food, a sirloin steak and a baked potato and salad on the side. The routine prayer is said, then it's time to dig in. He hears his mother blather away, but Rusty isn't listening. His mind wanders off inevitably to Carla, as he saws away at his steak.

"Rusty, is something the matter?"

Rusty stops what he's doing, his insides clenching up. A tear has run down his right cheek, and his mother has noticed it. His father has stopped eating and sits frozen by his side. "Nothing," Rusty mutters, though he knows his response is not going to cut it. He has to think of something right now. "I was just thinking about Larry."

Rusty's mother reaches across the dinner table and takes his hand. "I'm so sorry. I know this has been such a tough time for you!" Rusty appreciates her gesture, even if she doesn't know the true reason for his tears.

His father continues to sit silently at the table. He never asks about the letter.

1985

SEPTEMBER 1985

Peter "Rusty" Rassmussen, a college graduate and a recently hired social worker, sits in a smelly and heavily graffitied New York City subway car, enduring its deafening roar followed by the nails-on-the-chalkboard sound of squealing breaks as the train heads downtown from his job at Goldwater Memorial Hospital. As he has done for the last two months, he stares in awe at his fellow straphangers. After a lifetime of growing up in racially homogenous communities and being educated in a mainly white college, he continues to be amazed at the extreme diversity that is the Big Apple.

Many of his fellow riders, regardless of race or ethnicity, are in their own world, lost in whatever music playing in their headphones via their Walkmans. Rusty envies them. Right now, the song that's playing in his head is "Walking on Sunshine," by Katrina and the Waves. Rusty hates that song. A relentlessly happy and upbeat tune, it has been overplayed all summer, and Rusty is not into happy and upbeat music. His tastes in popular music involve songs about loss, heartbreak, and uncontrollable desire. He'd rather hear "Against the Odds" by Phil Collins, or "Missing You" by John Waite.

A few other straphangers have their faces buried in newspapers, mainly *The Post,* or *The Daily News.* Rusty prefers *The New York Times.* The news story that most fascinates him today is the discovery of the wreck of the Titanic in the bottom of the Atlantic Ocean. Of all the shipwrecks in human history, this is the one that captures his imagination. Maybe it's because it was advertised as "unsinkable," only to go down on its maiden voyage. Some of the passengers aboard were wealthy and famous. Maybe it's because there were not enough lifeboats, and that the available lifeboats weren't filled to capacity. What a fuckup.

He has since learned that the searchers in their submersible were actually quite close to the wreck at times but somehow missed it until now. Rusty can't help seeing a metaphor here, that real life is a series of near misses with serendipity and catastrophe, with the occasional direct hit with one or the other. Sometimes you find the sunken treasure, and sometimes you're the poor schmuck who hits the iceberg, and down you go.

As he has explained to his therapist, a kindly bearded Reiki master named George, whom Patti recommended, and whom he has just started seeing, his struggle for the past six years has been to "fill the hole," left by Larry's death and Carla's absence, through schoolwork and sports, alcohol and drugs, and by sleeping with many willing girls.

It hasn't gone very well for him.

After his sophomore year in high school, Rusty managed to find some success in running, particularly during his senior year, placing 3rd at the state indoor championships in the 1000 meters, and 2nd at the 800 in the state outdoor meet, though he would never again defeat Trevor LeValle. His grades were good enough for him to get accepted to a social work program in a college in New Hampshire.

But he never hit his stride socially, because he could never open up to anyone. Rusty never found another friend like Larry. His love life has been no better. He briefly dated a couple of girls from other high schools. In college, Rusty's relationships with women were mostly a parade of alcohol-fueled, unsatisfying one-night stands. He did have a girlfriend during his junior year, a first-year student named Sharon, a short, buxom girl with a full mane of dark hair and intense brown eyes. He liked Sharon. He liked her a lot. But he wasn't in love, he was noncommittal about their future together, and this frustrated her and confused him, since she seemed a bit young to be pursuing a committed relationship. She eventually sacked him on the eve of his 21st birthday.

To cope with his loneliness and loss, Rusty turned to alcohol. As a student in an academically challenging program, Rusty knew he had to keep the partying under wraps. He would stay off the bottle during the week, but come Friday and Saturday night, Rusty would sometimes drink himself to sickness, blackouts, and epic hangovers. Usually, he had fun with his weekend partying, but there were other times he could be a morose drunk, staggering off alone to some remote area where he would weep over Carla and Larry.

During those years he scarcely told anyone about Carla, and no one at all in his family until the summer before his final year in college. His sister, Patti, invited him to spend a week with her on Nantucket, where she had rented two rooms in a bed and breakfast. During his week with Patti, he listened in shock as she told him of her conflicts with their parents, her sexual promiscuity, failed relationships, her alcohol and drug use, and her frustration and pain over not being able to get decent acting work.

As Rusty listened to her day after day, he felt he could trust her with his secret, since she was clearly trusting him with all of hers. Finally, toward the end of the week, over dinner, Rusty told her. Her response surprised him. "Oh, please, I knew it. I knew you were full of shit, and I knew it all along," she said dismissively. "I could tell by your facial expression and your body language that you were lying and that you'd been fucking her." Rusty found himself bursting into uncontrolled laughter, partly due to the cabernet he was drinking, but mainly due to her profane and dismissive response. It was laughter so intense that it led to tears, and him nearly falling off his chair. They were tears of relief.

* * * * *

As Rusty progressed toward graduation, he wondered about where he wanted to pursue his social work career. He wanted to live someplace where he could meet a lot of young people like himself, and that had plenty of things to do. As it happened, Patti's roommate was getting married and moving out of the apartment in Manhattan that they shared. It was a rent-stabilized apartment in Stuyvesant Town, a nice neighborhood.

Rusty's opinion of New York City had changed greatly since high school. Just before graduating, he briefly dated a girl from Soho whom he had met at a beach party in Connecticut. She took him to Washington Square Park, where he saw the legendary street comic Charlie Barnett perform. Rusty found Barnett's raunchy routine funny. But what really fascinated him was the overall vibe of the park; the hippies, performers, exhibitionists, druggies, tourists, everyone. Rusty's interest in the city would be cemented the following year when Patti got him a summer job at the company where she worked.

Rusty discovered that social work was in high demand in the city. After graduating and obtaining his state license, he was able to find a position at Goldwater Hospital, a facility on Roosevelt Island. He primarily works with AIDS patients. He interviews them during their initial placement, finding out what their needs are, and what sort of family support they might have. Many suffer from depression and gradually increasing dementia, a result of the virus attacking the brain cells, causing patients to lose their minds "an inch at a time," in the words of a fellow staff member. Some of his patients admit to thoughts of suicide, but more often they talk of refusing further treatment.

For those patients who have already been in the facility, Rusty stops by their rooms and chats with them. The purpose of these informal meetings is to see if they are ready to settle their affairs while they are mentally able. This is difficult, since most of Rusty's clients are not gay men from middle class backgrounds, but intravenous drug users who have long ago burned their bridges with their families.

For patients who are in their final stages of illness, Rusty contacts their families to alert them, so they can pay their final visits. For those without families, he arranges to have aides sit at their bedside, so they won't die alone.

The work is emotionally draining, yet it gives Rusty a sense of purpose he has never known before. He has an ability to connect with his clients without coming across as judgmental, an important trait when dealing with an illness with so much social stigma. Rusty has discovered that they don't fear death; they fear the process of dying. They desperately want to be reassured that they won't die painful deaths, and that they won't die alone.

To deal with the stresses of the job, Rusty has returned to his old sport of running. He began by jogging in Central Park before he was due at work. His original goals were modest, get back into shape, maybe find a 5K or a 10K race somewhere. One day he was out running when he heard footsteps approaching behind him. The runner then stayed right behind for a few moments before coming to his side. For a moment, Rusty thought that he was about to get jumped. The stranger asked, "Excuse me, didn't you run for Northfield High a few years ago?" Startled, Rusty turned to the stranger.

"Yes, and you're Trevor Lavelle!" Rusty found out that Trevor was working in the city selling copiers. Rusty could tell that Trevor was a good salesman. Within a few minutes, he talked Rusty into joining his running club, and into running the New York City Marathon with him in November. Trevor occasionally trains with them on early morning runs in Central Park, after the muggers have finished plying their evening trades, trying desperately to keep up with them as they run endless miles at paces unimaginable during his high school days.

Since his breakup with Carla, he became much more serious about the guitar, renewing his musical partnership with Kevin, working on technique with Travis, and squeezing as much time as his studies and other commitments allowed, even writing a few of his own songs. Sometimes, he journeys down to Greenwich Village with his guitar to play the occasional open mic at some small coffeehouse or bar. Rusty's songs are all angst-ridden tunes about death, and loss of friendship or love. As a songwriter, Rusty is no Bob Dylan. His singing voice is good, but not great. But as a guitarist and overall performer, he is quite good, with a certain stage presence. Rusty is no longer the scrawny kid he was back in high school. He stands tall on stage, dressed in a black tank top and blue jeans, the muscles in his arms and shoulders, honed by years of working out in gyms, outlined by the spotlights overhead. He never gets booed and occasionally gets some decent applause.

Rusty's musical interests are further ignited by the scores of nightclubs that abound in Manhattan. He regularly checks the listings in the *Village Voice*, and sometimes acting on Patti's recommendation, journeys off to hear bands in clubs like Tramps, The Bottom Line, The Lone Star Roadhouse, and The Rodeo Bar.

But what he really loves to do during his spare time, what he can't seem to stop doing, is simply to roam the streets of the city and check out various bars, museums, record stores and bookshops. So far, Rusty's wanderings have largely been confined to lower Manhattan: Greenwich Village, the East and West Villages, and Soho. Sometimes he might check out the Mafia hangouts in Little Italy, or head over to Chelsea. But the village always sucks him back in, like a black hole in the heavens from which not even light can escape.

He frequently returns to Washington Square Park to check out the busking musicians and troupes of Black kids break dancing to Mellie Mel's "White Lines."

Rusty can sometimes spend an hour or so at Tower Records, browsing through the LPs, CDs and cassette tapes that are available, sometimes walking away with an armful of newly purchased albums. He also spends time and money in the small bookstores in the Village.

There is still a lot that bothers him about the city. The crime rate is skyrocketing, thanks in part to the crackheads breaking into cars and apartments with abandon, the pathetic "no radio" signs on car windows a testament to their reign. Due to his now well-trained eyes, Rusty is also witness to the gradual decimation of the gay community. He can now spot them from across the street, the young men with the gaunt skeletal faces and tell-tale purple Kaposi's Sarcoma lesions, the cardinal signs of full-blown AIDS. But despite all the crime and disease, the city has a vibrancy that Rusty loves. What he really hopes is that his time in the city will help lay to rest the ghosts that have haunted him for the past six years.

Rusty gets off at the Union Square station and begins his wanderings in Greenwich Village. He never goes straight home from work. Instead, he walks aimlessly around, occasionally ducking into a bar for a beer or two, or into a bookstore or a record shop, to browse, and also to check out any female customers who might also be shopping. Why bother with the flicks in Times Square when there is so much beauty to look at here? Every now and then a girl might return his gaze. This town really has promise.

He turns onto a street and sees a bookstore up ahead. It's The Strand, a bookstore he's been to many times before, since it's so close to Union Square. He looks at all the posters outside the store, advertising readings by obscure authors, when he freezes right there on the sidewalk. Despite the hot, fetid air, he feels a chill course through his body.

He reads "Carla Levy, 'Age of Consent,' September 7th, 8:00 PM."

Rusty stands at the door and feels a constriction in his chest. He becomes short of breath. An inner voice tells him, you're not breathing. He inhales, but by the time he does so, he's lost his balance, and his backside collides with a fellow pedestrian who's behind him. "Watch where you're going!" the man growls.

"Sorry, sir," Rusty gasps. He stares again at the poster, to make sure he's not dreaming or hallucinating and then looks at his watch. Today's the 6th, so it's on for tomorrow. He has passed by the store every working day this week and failed to notice the poster. All those near misses.

And now it all sinks in. They found the Titanic in the bottom of the Atlantic, and now I've found Carla, right here in New York City.

* * * * *

An hour later, holding a bag of groceries, Rusty inserts the key into the door of the 2nd floor apartment he shares with Patti. He enters the apartment and walks over to the living room, where he sees Patti sitting on the sofa, reading a *Village Voice*. She looks at him and blinks. "You look like you've just seen a ghost."

"In a way, I have."

"Oh? Do tell!" she replies, putting down her *Village Voice*, her eyebrows raised in anticipation.

Rusty puts the bag of groceries down on a counter, strides over to the sofa, and sits down next to her. "It appears that my old girlfriend from high school is alive and well, and is publishing her first novel. Or memoir. Or thinly disguised novel."

"The teacher girl?"

"Yep, that one."

"How did you find out?"

Rusty explains about his visit to the bookstore.

"Are you sure it's her?" she asks.

"Oh, it's her all right. Who else can it be? Wait, I forgot to tell you the title. It's called 'Age of Consent.'"

Patti bursts out into raucous laughter. "Oh man, you know what that means?"

"No, what?"

"You are her muse!"

"Huh, well that's only fair," he replies. "Many of my songs are about her."

"So, are you going to go?" she asks, suddenly serious.

"If I'm her muse, and she is mine, how can I not?"

"Right, how are you going to play it?"

"What do you mean?" asks Rusty.

"Well, you know she'll probably freak out when she sees you. Don't you want to hear her story first?"

Rusty considers this. She has a point. "Yeah, I do."

"It might be tough to walk in unnoticed, particularly if only a few people show up for her reading," Patti points out. "Most readings I've been to don't have huge turnouts, unless the author is famous. I wouldn't come early, if it were me."

Rusty takes this in. He's glad he can talk to Patti about this. "Yeah, you're right. The thing is, I really do want to hear her voice. Not just her physical voice. I want to hear what she has to say. About us."

* * * * *

There's no way he's getting any sleep tonight either. He gets up and heads to his bedroom, deciding to listen to some music. He knows what he wants to hear, and he pulls out from his expanding LP collection Bruce Springsteen's *Born in the USA*.

For many years, Rusty wasn't a big Springsteen fan. He thought he was okay, there were a couple of songs he rather liked, but he didn't love him the way some of his high school and college friends did.

All this changed with *Born in the USA*, which came out the previous year. Most rock albums have two or three good songs, the rest being mainly filler. This album has the opposite ratio, mostly excellent tunes and scarcely any filler.

However, Rusty has no intention of playing the whole album. He fishes out the record from its sleeve and sets it on the turntable. He puts on and plugs in his headphones, so he won't disturb Patti. He turns on the record player, and places the needle on side one, track six: "I'm on Fire."

It is not a typical Springsteen tune, with its soft, mellow rockabilly beat and use of synthesizers. What draws Rusty to this song are the lyrics. He takes a swallow from the wine, while taking in the melody, and listens to Springsteen ask his object of desire if her man is home, or if he had left her all alone.

Then comes the bridge. Rusty hears Springsteen sing of a knife cutting a six-inch valley into his soul, and of waking up in soaking wet sheets, and freight trains running through the middle of his head.

My god, how many fucking nights? How many times have I woken up that way? Almost every damned night, really. There were rare times, when he was with Sharon, in her arms, when the fire for Carla was contained. But it was never extinguished.

Rusty knows that it might not go well for him tomorrow night, and that he might come away with his heart utterly broken. She must have moved on, found another man, and this scares him. Rusty suspects though, that regardless of tomorrow night's outcome, the fire for Carla will burn for the rest of his life.

* * * * *

Rusty sits alone in a bar just a block away from The Strand. He is allowing himself one beer to cope with the fear and tension. Rusty is glad that today is Saturday. He is quite sure he would not have been able to focus on his job. The drawback is that this day has lasted for an eternity. He looks at his watch. Five to eight. Time to go.

Rusty downs the remnants of his beer, stands up, and heads for the door. Once outside, he feels short of breath, so he focuses on his breathing, in through the nose, out through the mouth. As he approaches the store, he feels the temptation to turn around and walk away. It reminds him of the time when he approached Coach Scarpella's office right after his meeting with the cop and principal. That didn't go badly, he reminds himself. So he continues on until he reaches the Strand's entrance. He stands at the threshold for a moment, takes a deep breath, and opens the door.

To Rusty's nearly simultaneous shock and relief, the bookstore is packed with people. Rusty wonders if Carla has a huge literary following or if it's because a large number of friends and family have shown up. Rusty suspects the latter; many of the women are brunette or have brown hair, with hourglass figures like Carla. Rusty is happy for her. No writer wants to read to an empty room.

Rusty looks around and sees a line leading to a cashier. A small stack of books stands at her table. Rusty suspects that these are copies of Carla's book. Rusty again looks around. The tallest man here is about six feet even, and scarcely anyone has blond hair. A six-foot three guy with red hair will stand out. Nonetheless, he sees that the number of copies available are dwindling fast. He decides to chance it and gets in line.

Within a minute, Rusty feels someone poking him in the shoulder, and he hears a stammering voice say "Um, um, um, ex...excuse me?"

A small, slim brunette in her fifties looks up at Rusty, smiling. There is something about her, the twinkle in her eyes perhaps, a certain charm that draws Rusty in, and he finds himself at ease despite the tension he's been feeling. An involuntary smile crosses his lips as he says "Yes?"

"Do you know Carla?" she asks. She speaks in an English accent.

"Uh, um, uh...a little bit. A long time ago," he stammers. *Idiot, you should have told her no.*

Suddenly serious, the woman says, "Well, I'm glad you're here and that there is such a great turnout for her reading. I'm her mother, you see, and I edited it and gave her advice. Carla is a very talented writer with a lot of interesting and original observations, but I want you to know, I don't agree with everything she says or does."

Rusty is feeling faint, and he can only imagine his current facial skin color. "Okay..." he says, drawing out the word for at least a couple of seconds.

"But, but, but, what I wanted to tell you was this," she continues, brightening up once again. "I saw you walking in, and I wanted to tell you, having worked on her novel, that you look just like the love interest of the protagonist, exactly the way Carla describes him!"

"Really?" replies Rusty, trying to feign innocence. The woman smiles and nods her head rapidly. "Well, then, I must have a literary twin, if not a literal one." She throws her head back and lets out a rapid ha-ha-ha laugh that one associates with Brits of a certain class.

"Next!" A girl behind the counter is impatiently alerting Rusty that he is now in the front of the line.

"Yes, I would like to buy this," he says, holding a copy of Carla's novel. The transaction complete, he turns. Carla's mother is gone. For a moment, Rusty considers bolting, but he sees bookshelves where he can hide. Looking downward, he hurries toward them without further incident.

"Okay, everyone," a woman's voice shouts. "Everybody find a seat so we can get the reading started!" As people move to take their seats, Rusty remains hiding in the bookshelves. He looks at his copy of Carla's novel, turns it over to the back and sees a beautiful head shot. Her face has matured some: she no longer has the look of someone fresh out of college. Well, she's thirty now, Rusty reminds himself.

"I want to thank you all for coming," says the woman who is apparently running the event. "What a great turnout! I want to introduce to you a new writer who has written a novel about a teacher who has fallen in love with a male student, told from her point of view. It's a bold, daring and original story..."

Bold, daring and original. I bet it is. Rusty opens up the book toward the beginning. He sees a page that is blank save for two words.

For Rusty.

"Oh, Jesus!" He's said it aloud, and a stooped elderly woman gives him an irritated look. "Sorry," Rusty mumbles. He looks down again at the page. Something about seeing his name on the page has caused the enormity of it all to sink in. Once again, he feels dizzy and short of breath. He grabs onto one of the shelves and takes a couple of deep breaths.

"Please welcome Carla Levy!"

As the audience applauds, Rusty peeks around the shelf and sees Carla wearing a form fitting sun dress showing a hint of cleavage. Her shoulder length brown hair is still curly, though not frizzy as it sometimes could be during warmer and more humid days.

She is still Carla.

"Thank you. I'm going to read from an early chapter. After meeting with a faculty member, my protagonist sees the student she eventually falls in love with get involved in a fight in the hallway. His name is Russell."

Rusty initially watches her read but has to look away. This is because she is well prepared and reads well, only occasionally looking down at her book before looking directly at the audience. Rusty does not want to be spotted, not now.

Carla reads of a tense meeting with a Mr. Kalish, who is the boy's cross-country coach, so he is the Mr. Kirschner character. To Rusty's amusement, she describes him as having a strong, foul body odor. After a few minutes, she leaves him and is walking down a hallway when she observes what appears to be a confrontation between a group of jocks and a helpless kid. Russell is there looking on. He's not going to do anything, she thinks. But then he steps in.

That's how it all started. That's how I entered her radar.

Carla concludes her reading and is rewarded with sustained applause. The organizer announces that Carla will be signing copies of her novel, so those who want their copy signed should line up now. Rusty watches as people begin to line up. He is not about to join the queue until he knows that he'll be the last person, because he knows that this will be a profound shock to Carla. *Let her enjoy her moment. I've waited six years for my moment. I can wait a little longer.*

While he waits, Rusty watches the people standing near Carla as she is signing away. He sees Carla's mother chatting with two much younger women, probably Carla's sisters. A bald-headed man with facial features nearly identical to Carla's is standing next to the mother, talking to other people. A very well-dressed gentleman is standing impassively near Carla, wearing what appears to be a suit by Armani. He looks at lot like the actor Richard Gere, back in his *American Gigolo* day. She said she didn't have any brothers. Rusty hopes he's a boyfriend of one of her sisters.

After about ten minutes, Rusty sees that no one else is joining the line, so he walks over and takes his place. Now the fear and tension return, and he occasionally takes deep breaths. There are twelve people ahead, yet he can hear Carla's voice as she accepts the congratulations, and with each person who steps away, the tension increases. Now there are eight people ahead. He sees Carla's mother look in his direction, so he looks down, trying to be inconspicuous, even though he is taller than anyone else here, especially the stooped old lady in front of him who shot him a look earlier. She is more than a foot shorter than Rusty. Four people ahead. The wait is becoming agony. He can hear every word exchanged between Carla and her readers. He thinks of the time he first saw Carla, when Mr. Kirschner introduced her to the cross-country team. Three people ahead. Rusty remembers the first time Carla chatted with him at the library, when she told him her first name. Two people ahead. Now he's backstage at the auditorium, watching her transcendent performance at the talent show. One person ahead. Rusty is fighting the urge to turn tail and run. He remembers their first kiss.

The stooped old lady in front of Rusty steps away, and now he is standing before her.

"Hello, Carla."

Carla cries, "Rusty! What are you doing here?"

Despite all the mental preparation for this event, Rusty is nearly shocked into silence. He mumbles, "Well, I live here. Work here, too."

"So, it *is* you," says her mother with a smile.

"Yes, it is, ma'am. I am Rusty. I'm sorry that I was evasive with you earlier. I wanted to wait until after she was done, because I knew this would be a shock."

Carla's mother nods her head in understanding.

A profound silence has descended, with most people staring agape, except for the two younger women who are likely Carla's sisters, who seem to stare approvingly. One of them asks "So, is that the kid Carla had the affair with?"

The other says, "Yeah, and now I see why."

Carla still sits in stunned silence, a hand covering her mouth. An engagement ring with a huge diamond rests on her finger, and Rusty is deflated. However, he keeps his composure. He has a plan B, and he decides to use it.

"Look Carla, I know this is pretty awkward. I got something I want to give you." He pulls out his wallet and takes out a business card. "Here, this is where I work, and this is my home phone," he says turning the card over. "I live and work right here in New York City, so you know where to find me." He places the card down on the table in front of her.

"Don't you dare take that card!" yells the American Gigolo.

"David!" snaps Carla.

So that's his name, Rusty notes. He turns and glares at David. "Sir, I am going to give her my card. She has every right to do whatever she wants with it." Turning back to Carla, he says "Look, if you don't want to call me, I understand, but I hope you will. Anyway," he continues, waving her novel, "I want to congratulate you. That's quite an accomplishment. I'm really looking forward to reading this." He turns around and is starting to walk out.

"Rusty!" Carla yells. He stops in his tracks and turns to face her. "I'll be in touch," she says. Her fiancé lets out a sigh of disgust. Rusty smiles.

"Okay," he says before turning and leaving.

When Rusty reaches the sidewalk, he pauses. *My God, what just happened here?* He looks down at his copy of Carla's novel, and realizing that he wants to continue reading it now, begins to run the long avenue blocks on 14th Street that eventually lead to his apartment.

When Rusty enters the apartment, he finds Patti watching TV. She asks, "Well, how did it go?"

"I did it," he says, brandishing the book. He tells her about the reading.

"Let's see," she commands. Rusty hands her the book. She looks at the back cover. "Well, she is pretty." She hands it back to him. "You did what you had to do, now the ball's in her court."

"Yup. Now if you'll excuse me, I've got to catch up on my reading."

There's no way he's getting any sleep tonight either. He's already read about a third of her novel when the phone rings. It's 11:15.

"Hello?"

"Rusty," a voice whispers. Wow, that didn't take long, he thinks happily.

"I must say you've written a real page turner."

"Wow! So, I guess you like it?"

"Like it? Love it is more like it. I've got a question, though. Did you really write that song about me?"

"Yes, I did."

"Why didn't you tell me?"

Carla sighs. "I guess I didn't want to scare you away."

"There wasn't much danger of that."

"Oh, Rusty." Carla sighs again.

"I want to see you," says Rusty. "How about I buy you a drink, right now, to celebrate?" There is silence on the other end. Shit, I went too far. She's engaged. The guy might be with her right now. He blurts out "Hey, I'm of age now, I can do that, you know!" Rusty is rewarded with laughter on the other end.

"Okay," she says. "Where is home for you now?"

"I'm in Stuyvesant Town, 14th and Avenue A."

"I'm in the West Village. Morton Street and Bleecker."

"Okay. I know the village pretty well now."

"You know the arch at Washington Square Park? Meet me there in a half hour."

After Rusty bolts from his apartment, he has to fight the urge to run to the park, since she gave him a half hour to get there. The rational side of him knows that he has to tamp down his expectations. He finds himself walking at a brisk pace, though he slows down as he nears the park.

He sees Carla standing by the arch. She has changed clothes. Now she's wearing a tight, low-cut maroon tank top, and a tan mini skirt. She sure never dressed like that when she was teaching school. Rusty stands for a moment, taking her in. *You dress like that and you're engaged to another guy? Carla, you're killing me.*

Rusty walks toward her and calls out, "Carla!"

Seeing Rusty, she runs toward him. They embrace, and Rusty, feeling the contours of her body for the first time in six years, feels so strongly aroused that he wants to take her, right here in the park. Yet the arousal is mixed with sadness and pain, for now she belongs to another man.

Releasing her embrace, she looks up at Rusty. "Wow, just look at you. You have really come into your own!"

"You look pretty good yourself."

"Thank you," Carla says smiling. "Let's go find a cafe," she suggests.

As they begin to walk together, she asks, "So, what do you do in the city? I see you're working in a hospital?"

"Yes." Rusty tells her about his work. As he does so, he sees Carla's face become progressively sad, her eyes brimming with tears. After he finishes, he asks, "Is something the matter?"

"Oh, Rusty," she says while wiping away a tear. "I'm so proud of you. You really are living up to the ideal of trying to make the world a better place. I just wish I was doing the same."

"Actually, in a way, you have," Rusty counters. "Do you remember that time when we were sitting at my backyard, and you suggested that I should be a social worker? Sounds like you would have been a great guidance counselor!"

Carla laughs at this. "Glad I could help you out in directing you toward a career." After a pause, she asks, "What do you do in your spare time?"

"Well, a number of things. Remember when you talked me into doing that talent show, and I told you I'm not a solo performer?"

"Yeah?"

"I've written some songs, and I actually perform them sometimes."

"Really? Where?"

"Just some open mics in little places in the Village."

"I want to hear you perform! You must tell me when you're playing next. Promise?"

"Sure, I just need your phone number."

"I'll give it to you. Don't you worry about that." She points at a café. "Look, Rusty, an empty outside table. Do you want to have a drink here?"

"Sure." They each take a seat. A waitress appears, and Rusty orders champagne for both. After she leaves, Rusty says, "So, tell me about your life for the past six years."

"Okay," begins Carla. "Well, after I left Northfield, I decided that I was done with being a teacher. Eventually, I landed a sales job. I sell ad space for a publisher that puts out trade journals for scientists. Much of my work is on the phone, but it also requires some travel. My territory is the central time zone, so it's anywhere from New Orleans to Minneapolis."

"Sounds like fun."

"Well, New Orleans is fun."

Rusty takes a breath. "So, tell me about the gentleman you're with."

"His name is David. We met two years ago through some mutual friends."

"What does he do?"

"He's an investment banker. He works for First Boston."

"Wow, he's got money."

"Well, yes," Carla admits, blushing. "Anyway, he's Jewish, like me. My mom likes him enough. My dad, not so much. A little too capitalist for his taste."

The waitress arrives with the drinks. Rusty raises his glass in a toast. "To the success of your first novel." After taking his first swallow of champagne, Rusty says "Well, if this David has any heart, he'll let you quit your job, so you can be a full-time writer."

"Yes, maybe." After a pause she says, "He's nice." A look of profound sadness crosses her expressive face.

He's nice? What the hell does that mean? He's about to ask her about that, but Carla quickly regains her footing. "So, what about you?"

"What about me?"

"Do you have a girlfriend?"

Oh, God. Rusty would rather undergo a root canal than tell Carla about his personal life the past six years. "Actually, before I answer that, I have an unanswered question. It's something I've been wondering about for the past six years."

"Okay," she says, looking both wary and surprised.

"How the hell did anyone find out about us? I never said anything to anybody. And when I got hauled out of class by Mr. Hessman, I lied to the police, I lied to the principal, I lied to my parents, I lied to my friends, I lied to my enemies. I lied to the world!"

An expression of embarrassment and guilt cross her face as she looks down. "It was my fault, Rusty. I did something really, really stupid. I told my roommate, and she reported me. That bitch."

Rusty leans back in his chair, and slumps as he absorbs this. "I always thought there was something hostile about her. I guess she thought you were abusing your position, violating a trust, corrupting a minor... "

"It sounds like you're taking her side," says Carla.

"No, I'm not. Just trying to get into her head, that's all. 'Real life bad guys don't think they're being bad guys.' Remember? You told me that once."

"Maybe you shouldn't have listened to me so much."

"I hung on to every word you said to me back then. Anyway, I'm not too surprised about your roommate. I came by your place after you left, and I met her. It didn't go very well." He tells her of his desperate bike ride down to Norwalk.

Carla appears both sad and disturbed for a moment, but she regains her composure. Managing a smile, she asks, "Do you have any other questions?"

"No, that's it," says Rusty, smiling back.

"Well, I have to confess something," says Carla. "I came by your house a couple of times after I left."

"What? When did you do that?"

"First time was in late June."

"Late June, let me see. Oh yes, my mom and I were in Illinois, visiting our relatives."

"The second time was in early August," Carla says.

Rusty is now truly aghast. "We were on vacation then, down in the Smoky Mountains of North Carolina and Tennessee. God damn, I'm so sorry I missed you! What bad luck. After I got your letter, I would try to look you up every time I got my hands on a Manhattan phone book. I thought of calling up every number that was listed as 'Levy C,' but I chickened out. Your letter was postmarked New York City, so I figured you had ended up here.

Carla lets out a sad smile. "So, what's with you? Do you have a girlfriend?"

Oh fuck, here we go. "No."

"Have you been dating anyone since you started living here?"

"No."

"How about before?"

Feeling very uncomfortable, Rusty shifts in his seat. "Well, yeah, I dated some girls in high school and college, but nothing really serious. I did have a girlfriend during my junior year in college. We went out for a couple of months, but we broke up."

Carla's facial expression darkens. "You know Rusty, I worry sometimes that maybe I hurt you, maybe even damaged you."

"Well, look, it's true that my life went completely to hell when you left, but it wasn't just you. My best friend committed suicide. That was pretty fucking huge."

"I know, I know. Still, I feel a lot of guilt. I want you to feel free to be honest with me. You've just told me that you haven't had any long relationships with girls. If I hurt you in some way..."

"Okay you can stop right now!" he snaps. An inner levee has broken within Rusty, and now he can't stop himself. "I mean, I get it, okay?"

"What?" asks a stunned Carla.

"I know where this is going. I know what you're going to say to me. You're over me, you've met this rich handsome guy that you're truly, madly, deeply in love with..."

"No!"

"You're going to get married and live happily ever after and I'm supposed to accept it and be happy for you, and now I'm supposed to grow up, get over it, and find myself a proper girl, an appropriate girl, a virginal Roman Catholic girl instead of a Jewish red diaper baby who's older than me, with whom I can have two or three kids, the house, the two car garage, the white picket fence, and maybe a dog and a cat, the American dream, right? Because you just want to be friends."

"No!" Carla nearly screams, turning the heads of fellow nearby patrons.

"No? Noooo? Then why are you so interested in my personal life? You want to know if I've been sleeping with other women since you left? Yeah, I've been with other girls, okay? That's not the problem!" He slams his hand down on the table.

"What is the problem?" asks Carla.

Rusty bursts into an angry, mirthless laughter. He shakes his head. "You don't want to know the answer to that."

"It's okay," Carla says leaning forward. "If you feel that I've hurt you, or harmed you in any way, I want you to tell me."

Rusty now feels completely backed into a corner. She wants the truth. "Okay," he says. "Okay, I'll tell you. Brace yourself." Rusty suddenly feels the urge to cry. He takes a deep breath and says, "About that college girlfriend I just told you about, her name is Sharon, by the way. Anyway, toward the end of our relationship, she accused me of being in love with another woman. She did! And you know something, she was right. I'm guilty as charged. And if you're at all interested in the identity of the other woman, all you have to do is take a long look at yourself in the mirror." Rusty sees a solitary tear descend on Carla's cheek. "I'll tell you something else, and I really shouldn't be telling you this, but hey, you keep asking. Whenever I have been with another girl, as in really with another girl, the only way I can go through with it is by pretending that she's you. I have never, ever been able to let you go, and I just don't think I ever will."

Rusty can't bear to look at Carla anymore. He buries his face in his hands. Oh God, this is it. This is when she delivers the coup de grace. Like a passenger on a doomed aircraft, he braces for the impact.

"You have no idea what I'm going to say to you," Carla says. "You don't have a clue."

A long pause, as Rusty braces himself further.

She cries out, "I'm in the same boat as you!"

Rusty looks up in shock as Carla dissolves into tears. Now he feels remorse. "Carla, I'm so sorry. I..."

"It's true! I dedicated my fucking novel to you." After a pause, she adds more quietly, "Whenever I've been with another man, I find myself wishing he was you."

Rusty now has this one last question to ask her. In a quiet, tremulous voice he asks, "Even now?"

Carla doesn't say anything, perhaps because she can't. She closes her eyes, and fresh tears run down her cheeks as she nods her head.

She's already ruined her life because of me once before, Rusty thinks. *There's no fucking way she's going to do that again.*

And then, the next thought that comes to Rusty's mind is...Doug Flutie, the Heisman-winning quarterback from Boston College.

This is not the time to be thinking about football. It's just wrong. But he can't help it. He thinks about that final play that Thanksgiving weekend, when Flutie threw that ball with all his might in his final effort to win the game. The ball ended up sailing in the air over 63 yards, into a 30 mile per hour headwind, toward a goal line populated by many Miami defenders, each with perfectly good sets of hands that could either intercept or bat away the ball and seal Flutie's fate.

Except that one set of hands rose behind all the others, and those belonged to Gerard Phelan, Flutie's star receiver.

It was just a football game. But sometimes, real life can bring situations that call for the desperation play.

Rusty straightens up in his seat and takes a deep breath. "Carla, I have some things I want to tell you."

Carla stops sobbing and straightens up in her chair. She looks directly at Rusty.

"First of all, I'm not 16 years old anymore. I'm 22. I'm an adult, just like you! And obviously, I'm not in high school anymore. I'm a college graduate, and I'm out in the world. Now, it's true, I'm not a wealthy investment banker. That's not who I am, and that's not who I'm going to be. But I'm in a good job in my field, and I have to say, I think I'm doing okay at it. I'm not living at home with my parents anymore. Like I told you before, I live and work right here in the city. I'm single. And most importantly, way more important, I have longed for you, pined for you, yearned for you, and

I have missed you in ways you can't even imagine. And I know this sounds extreme, but given the way I've felt about you, and the way I feel about you now, I would gladly give up all the remaining years of my life just so I could spend my last few moments with you in my arms." Rusty leans back in his chair. "What do you say?"

For a few moments Carla sits still in her chair, staring at Rusty. Suddenly she stands up. *Oh god, I blew it. I went too far.* Still staring at Rusty, she grabs her chair, walks over to him and places the chair next to Rusty and sits down. She removes her engagement ring and places it on the table. "You don't have to give up anything for me, Rusty."

As they kiss, Rusty wonders how she's going to break it to her fiancé and her family. He has no idea about how he's going to explain this to his parents. But as they continue to embrace, Rusty thinks he just might give "Walking on Sunshine" another listen.

Hell, he might even buy the record.

ACKNOWLEDGEMENTS

Thank you to Naomi Rosenblatt, who encouraged me to write this book. And thanks to her team at Heliotrope Books: Jaime Lubin, Jen Maguire, and Tony Brescia.

www.ingramcontent.com/pod-product-compliance
Lightning Source LLC
Chambersburg PA
CBHW032150020726
47496CB00003B/807